"Might as well face it, Maureen. You've got the hots for me."

She went rigid. "I do not have—"

"And I've got the hots for you. Been that way since the day I met you. Why do you think we've fought so much?"

"Because you *stole* my daughter and grandson."

"Nope. It's chemistry. Big-time, never-flagging chemistry."

"Not for me."

Daniel smiled slowly, sexily. "Liar."

***

"*The Merry Widow's Diary* [by Susan Crosby] is full of touching details as Jill tries to build a new life. Her experiences with a grief support group are funny and affecting. All the characters shine, and Jill is heartwarming in her confusion as she tries to make a new life for herself."
—*Romantic Times BOOKreviews*

Susan Crosby

Susan Crosby believes in the value of setting goals, but also in the magic of making wishes. A longtime reader of romance novels, Susan earned a B.A. in English while raising her sons. She lives in the central valley of California, the land of wine grapes, asparagus and almonds. Her checkered past includes jobs as a synchronized swimming instructor, personnel interviewer at a toy factory and trucking company manager, but her current occupation as a writer is her all-time favorite.

Susan enjoys writing about people who take a chance on love, sometimes against all odds. She loves warm, strong heroes, good-hearted, self-reliant heroines…and happy endings.

Susan loves to hear from readers. You can visit her at her Web site, www.susancrosby.com.

I'M YOUR MAN

Susan Crosby

I'M YOUR MAN

copyright © 2007 by Susan Bova Crosby

isbn-13:978-0-373-88145-1

isbn-10:   0-373-88145-2

TheNextNovel.com

 HARLEQUIN®

PRINTED IN U.S.A.

From the Author

Dear Reader,

Some of the challenges in life are the unpredictable situations that pop up along the way, situations that surprise, mystify, even hurt us at the time, until we take a step back and see them for what they truly are. We grow up having certain expectations, believing there is an order to how things should happen. However, it rarely turns out the way we expect.

For my heroine, Maureen Hart, becoming a grandmother at thirty-four was as unexpected as having become a mother at seventeen. She learned, as many of us do, that something amazing happens when you become a grandparent, a joy no one can fully comprehend until it's personal. To complicate things, families used to stay put more, giving grandparents and grandchildren the chance to cement the bond that's so different from the parent/child relationship. But now families are often scattered around the country, even the world, and must rely on technology to keep them close.

I'm Your Man tells the story of this young grandmother who suddenly gets the opportunity to know her six-year-old grandson beyond phone calls, computer-camera connections and short visits. It also touches on the importance of forgiveness, moving on and self-acceptance.

Even more, it's about how love—as an unexpected gift from an unlikely place—can find you, even after you've decided it's never going to come your way.

I hope you enjoy her journey.

Susan Crosby

For Austin and Molly, who brighten my life in infinite ways.
And for Barbara, Chickie and Linda,
who soothe the savage beasts.

CHAPTER 1

Maureen Hart watched the glass cleaner drip down the bedroom window as she waited for someone to react, her back to the three other females in the room. Usually she spent the third Saturday of every month with the Rowdies, a group of girlfriends who descended on San Francisco's club-and-concert scene with all the restraint of teenagers on spring break. This third Saturday, however, the Rowdies were blowing off steam without her as Maureen helped the pregnant-and-bedridden Bonnie Sinclair instead.

"He gave you a key to his *house?*" Maureen's aunt Cherie repeated, her reaction sufficiently surprised. She had picked up her red Candy Land game piece but didn't move it to the next purple square on the path. "Did you accept it?"

Maureen attacked the wet window with paper towels. "I didn't know how not to."

The game came to a complete halt at the news that Maureen's boyfriend of five months, Ted Montague, had made a show out of giving her a key to his house, having wrapped it up like a present and smiling like a kid at Christmas as she opened it.

"Did you give him yours?" Cherie asked.

"I didn't have an extra one."

Cherie gave her an easily interpreted look.

"Well, I didn't," Maureen said.

"Are you *going* to?"

"I either have to or return his, don't I?"

"Play, please," ordered five-year-old Morgan, fidgeting on the queen-size bed.

Morgan's seven-months-pregnant, ordered-to-bed mother, Bonnie, brushed the girl's brown curls from her face and smiled. "Be patient, sweetheart. This is important information for later in your life."

Morgan sighed. "Bor-ing. Can I watch a movie?"

"Sure."

The girl climbed off the bed and skipped out of the room. Bonnie rubbed her hands together. "Now we can talk. Why don't you want to exchange keys, Maureen? You've been dating long enough, *and* you're taking a big vacation together. It's a natural step."

It was a fish-or-cut-bait step, Maureen thought, eyeing the clean window for streaks. Exchanging keys was only a step away from moving in together, a first in her thirty-nine years.

"I'm sorry," Bonnie said, subdued. "It's really none of my business."

"No, that's not it at all. I just don't have an answer."

Maureen set her cleaning supplies aside and sat on a chair next to the bed that Bonnie had called home for a week, and would continue to until she gave birth. "I'm sorting through how I feel."

Maureen's gaze drifted to the framed photograph on the nightstand of a handsome Navy lieutenant, Bonnie's husband of six years, now stationed in the Middle East, with six months left on his current tour. "Did you hear from Jeremy today?" Maureen asked.

"I got an e-mail. He was very upbeat. I know he doesn't want me to worry…."

An impossible task, Maureen thought, since Bonnie was confined to bed, unable to work, unable to do much of anything for herself or her daughter, which left a lot of time for thinking—and worrying. She had no family nearby, was dependent solely on public services and Cherie and Maureen, strangers until a week ago.

Morgan bounded back into the room, carrying several DVDs. With the efficiency of someone who'd grown up with the technology, she popped in a movie then climbed onto her mother's bed, remote control in hand.

"So, Bonnie," Cherie said as she put away the board game. "What else can we do before we leave?"

"Else? You've cleaned my apartment, top to bottom. You've stocked my refrigerator, given Morgan a bath, changed the bedding. I can't even list it all. There's nothing else. Thank you so much. Both of you."

"Gregor will bring your food tomorrow and Monday. By

Tuesday we should have a helper in place, at least for four or five hours a day. No word from your sister about coming to stay with you?"

"She's trying to work it out. She's got three kids of her own, you know. Everyone else has jobs they can't leave."

Can't or won't? Maureen wondered.

"I'll see you on Tuesday," Cherie said. "Just to make sure everything is working out. Call me if you need anything before then."

Everyone hugged goodbye. A minute later Maureen and Cherie went down the flight of stairs and left the building. Night hadn't quite fallen on the cool, breezy June day, a time of year Maureen loved, contrary to winter, when it was dark so early, making her bus ride home from work seem twice as long.

"I can't believe no one from Bonnie's family has come," Maureen said as they walked to her car. "Or Jeremy's for that matter. Why isn't anyone helping?"

"My guess? Bonnie's downplayed the seriousness of her condition."

"Well, that's ridiculous. Maybe I can sneak around a bit, find a phone number or two and give someone a nudge."

"You're getting attached," her aunt said with a smile as Maureen pulled away from the curb, agitated.

Maureen smiled back. "Guilty. I can't imagine being restricted like she is. I'm glad you found out about her. Glad we can help."

"Me, too."

Maureen admired her aunt more than anyone on earth. At seventy most people had slowed down a little. Cherie seemed to get busier. Retired from a forty-five-year career as a nurse, she now volunteered at a free clinic three mornings a week; delivered Mobile Meals three afternoons a week, a service she started herself five years ago when she retired, and worked at a soup kitchen on Sundays. She swam twice a week and walked almost everywhere. A petite five-two, she dressed in comfortable, trendy clothes and kept her hair colored and highlighted. She'd never married, but men doted on her. Most people did, actually. She sparkled like the silver peace symbol she always wore on a chain around her neck.

"Are you going to catch up with the Rowdies?" Cherie asked. "Seems like there's enough time."

"I'm tempted just to take a shower, slip into something comfortable and watch TV. It's been a long day. But…" Every Saturday Maureen acted as Cherie's driver to deliver meals to homebound people, starting at noon to pick up the prepacked meals from whichever restaurant was donating that particular day, until whatever time Maureen and Cherie finished delivering the meals and chatting with the recipients, who often didn't have other company.

"But?" Cherie prompted.

"But I hate to miss seeing the Rowdies. Kicking up my heels."

"How does Ted feel about your girls' night out?"

"He'd rather I spend the time with him, of course. I don't

let it bother me." *Much*. Maureen turned onto Cherie's street and double-parked in front of her house.

Cherie patted Maureen's cheek. "Thanks so much for going the extra mile for Bonnie."

She hugged her aunt, the woman who'd been most responsible for raising Maureen since her mother died when Maureen was five. "It's fun watching Morgan, especially since she's so close in age to Riley."

"I know it makes you miss him more, too."

Maureen nodded and said good-night. Yes, she missed her grandson, and her daughter, too, who lived in Seattle. Maureen led a full, busy life. She had a job she loved, was even up for promotion to vice president of operations. She had a boyfriend, her first long-term, steady boyfriend in years and years. She had her Saturday work with Cherie for Mobile Meals, which satisfied a deep need to nurture. But it wasn't the same as being with the people she loved most in the world.

Maureen's house was only a few blocks from Cherie's in the same Bernal Heights area of San Francisco. She parked her car in the garage she rented a few doors down from her own garageless house, then walked home.

Maybe she should invite Bonnie and Morgan to move in with her until the baby came. She had a guest room. And toys not being used by anyone....

The wrought-iron gate at the bottom of her stairway creaked when she opened it. The climb to her sweet little house seemed steeper than usual. Sometime soon she was going to find time for an exercise routine beyond her once-a-day ascent up one single flight....

Uh-huh. Sure. What other fantasies do you entertain?

"That Social Security will be viable when I retire," she muttered aloud. "That chocolate is a food group. That knights in shining armor exist."

Maureen fit her key into her front door and found it already unlocked. She froze. Had she locked it that morning? Of course she had. She never forgot to lock her door.

She turned the handle gingerly and eased open the door, then crept down the hallway to the living room, hearing voices. Heart hammering, she peeked around the corner and spotted her daughter and grandson watching television.

Shock gave way to pleasure, her heart pounding in a different way. She hadn't seen them in six months, since Christmas. "Looks like I need to call 9-1-1. Somebody broke into my house."

"We used Mommy's key!" her six-year-old grandson exclaimed, looking nervously at his mother.

Maureen laughed. "Well, it's not a crook, after all. It's my sweet Riley. C'mere, you." She crouched and opened her arms.

He finally smiled as he shyly approached her. His two front teeth were missing, giving him even more of an impish look than what she could see during their twice-weekly computer-video calls. Maureen kissed him, noting his shock of blond hair was spiked with gel, a new style for him. He looked adorable. Her heart swelled as she held him close. She wished he would relax against her. They'd had too little contact through the years, and had to rebuild their relationship every time they saw each other.

"Where did you come from?" she asked before she got mushy and embarrassed herself.

"From the car, silly."

"Can I get a hug, too?" came a hopeful voice.

"Jess, honey." Maureen reached for her beautiful daughter. She felt sturdy and strong, for all her slenderness. The rare pleasure of holding her daughter brought the sting of tears again. "What a wonderful surprise."

Jess was only a slightly darker blond than Riley, but they both had Maureen's green eyes, the only physical trait she seemed to have passed on to the next generations, which was okay by her. She'd been teased all her life about her red hair. "When did you get here?"

"Just a few minutes ago."

"We're having a 'venture," Riley said.

"You are? Are you going on a safari?"

"No, silly. We came to see *you!*"

"I'm so happy you did." Although curious…and wary. "You drove all the way from Seattle just to see me?" *Without calling first?*

"In only thirty-teen hours," Riley announced.

Maureen looked sharply at her daughter. Like Maureen, Jess had become a single mother at seventeen. Unlike Maureen, Jess hadn't been a model of responsibility.

"Thirteen," Jess corrected her son. "We made plenty of stops along the way, Mom."

The last thing Maureen wanted was an argument with her daughter, whom she usually saw only twice a year. "Are you hungry? Or thirsty?"

"Chocolate milk and chocolate chip cookies, please," Riley said.

"Plain milk will have to do, okay?" *If I'd known you were coming…*

"Okay."

She opened the cabinet where she kept toys for Riley's rare visits. He raced over and pulled out a basket of Hot Wheels, grabbing the three unopened packages on top. "Awesome! Mommy, look! Fire engines."

"Cool." Jess knelt to help him open the packages.

Maureen watched them for a few seconds. Something was up. Tension beyond the normal mother/daughter strain crackled in the air. Jess barely made eye contact, unusual for her. "In your face" was a term coined with Jess in mind.

"How about you, Jess?"

"Cookies and milk would be great, Mom. Thanks."

Maureen retreated to her cozy kitchen, her thoughts spinning. She glanced at the refrigerator, decorated with photos and crayon drawings. She touched a fingertip to last year's Christmas photo and the grins on their faces. Why had Jess come? What was happening? Since Jess had spirited Riley off to Seattle when he was just a few months old, she rarely initiated contact. Maureen had been the one to make plans to visit, to make ninety-five percent of the phone calls. She'd even bought them a computer with a video camera so that she and Riley could keep in touch more intimately than through phone calls.

Why are you here, Jess?

Maureen got her cookie plate down from her cupboard and took out a bakery box of the big, chewy, chocolate chip cookies she kept to satisfy Ted's sweet tooth, then poured two glasses of milk.

"I could use a little help," she called out, hoping to get a minute alone with her daughter, but it was Riley who popped into the kitchen.

"Those cookies are *big*," he said.

"Hmm. I think you're right. Maybe I should break them into smaller pieces and put some back?"

"No way." He grinned.

She handed him the plate, then picked up the glasses and followed him. They sat on the floor among a city of cars already in place.

"This is the dish that Mommy painted, huh, Grandma? I can read it now. It says, 'I love you, Mom.'"

"That's right. She made it for me when she was twelve years old, for Mother's Day." *When I was still a cool mom to her.*

Jess slid her fingers around the circle of multicolored hearts painted around the edge. "Aunt Cherie took me to a do-it-yourself ceramics shop. We had a blast."

"I wanna do that," Riley mumbled, cookie crumbs spraying.

"Swallow before you talk, bud."

Maureen took advantage of the opportunity. "Maybe the shop is still in business. How long are you staying?"

"I'm not sure yet, Mom."

"No idea? A day? A week? A month?" she added in a teasing tone.

"I really don't know."

An open-ended visit? Now Maureen was really worried.

A long silence followed, until Riley finished his cookie and yawned. "Mommy, I'm tired."

"Of course you are, bud. Let's get you to bed."

Maureen opened the sleeper-sofa in the guest room while Jess supervised Riley's bedtime preparations. Hugs and kisses followed. His stuffed tiger, Stripe, was tucked in with him. He was almost asleep before the light was turned out.

"I'm going to bed, too," Jess said outside the guest room door. "I'm wiped."

She headed toward the bathroom, but Maureen stopped her. "What's going on?"

"What do you mean?"

"I mean you drive all the way down here without calling first. What if I'd been gone?"

"You're never gone."

Maureen had no response to that. Jess was right. It was a bone of contention with Ted, too. Which was why she'd finally given in and scheduled a vacation.

"Jess—"

"Really, Mom, I'm exhausted. Can we talk later?"

"I guess so." What else could she say?

Jess slipped into the bathroom and shut the door.

Maybe it would be good to wait until tomorrow anyway.

Since they pushed each other's buttons easily, having a full night's sleep first could only help.

By the time Maureen cleaned up the kitchen it was a little after ten o'clock. She climbed into bed and dialed Ted's number.

"Guess what I came home to?" she said when he answered.

"An empty house with no one to rub your feet."

She smiled. "That's true. And in retrospect…"

"I can be there in ten minutes." When she didn't encourage him, he said, "I give up. What did you come home to?"

"My daughter and grandson." She filled him in.

"It's hard to imagine someone coming that far without checking to see if it was okay."

"It's also so Jess. She's always been impulsive. I wouldn't be surprised to learn she got up early this morning and decided on a whim to come." *But what does she want? Because there has to be a catch….*

"She knows we're leaving for Europe in two weeks, right?"

"We really didn't get to talk." A long silence ensued. "Maybe we all could go on a picnic tomorrow. It would be a great way for you to get to know each other, in a casual situation like that."

"Sure. I'll come around noon."

"Good. Gives me time to shop first."

"How come you got home so early from your girls' night?" he asked.

"Cherie and I ended up staying at Bonnie's place a lot

longer. She needed quite a bit done. I came home to change my clothes and go back out, but then Jess and Riley were here."

"Lucky timing."

"It sure was."

After they hung up she lay in bed, too keyed up, too curious and too, well, happy. She shouldn't question why Jess had come but just be grateful. Maybe Jess was reaching out. Maybe at twenty-three she was finally maturing.

Maybe second chances could happen, after all.

Then again, maybe it was just something to add to her list of fantasies.

CHAPTER 2

As much as Maureen wanted to sleep in, her internal alarm woke her at 6:00 a.m. Frustrated, she pulled the blanket higher and rolled over—and came almost nose to nose with Riley, who stood beside her bed, solemn-faced, staring at her. Her heart thumped at the surprise, but she calmly said good morning.

"Here." He shoved an envelope at her.

Dread slammed into Maureen. She sat up and patted the spot beside her, inviting Riley to join her. He didn't budge, except to tighten his hold on his tiger. His eyes brightened with tears.

She opened the letter.

Dear Mom,
I'm sorry to just take off like this, but I couldn't let you talk me out of leaving. I'm going to be on *True Grit!* It's a reality TV show, and the winner gets a million dollars. I'm going to win. I just know it.

The filming takes about six weeks. You won't be able to get in touch with me unless it's an emergency.

I attached a sheet of instructions from the show's producers and the legal forms you need if you have to authorize medical care for Riley. I won't be allowed to call home. I have no idea where I'll be.

I know you don't think I'm responsible, Mom, but I can do this. I can win it. Then I'll have enough money to be independent and take care of Riley by myself. It's for him, Mom. He'll also need money for college, and this is the best chance I have of getting it. And it's time for me to go out on my own, not rely on Daniel anymore.

So I'm leaving Riley with you. You've always said you've been cheated out of knowing him because I took him to live at Daniel's. Now's your chance.

Have fun with my baby.

Love, Jess

P. S. I've enclosed a blank journal. I'd appreciate it if you would jot things down, you know, the Rileyisms he's famous for, so that I don't feel like I've missed so much time with him. Thanks!

"She went away," Riley said, his lower lip quivering. "She's not coming back for a long, long time. Forever!"

Against his protests, Maureen lifted him into bed and tucked him close. Jess, Jess, Jess. What have you done? And why me instead of Daniel? "Did Mommy tell you where she's going, honey?"

He nodded, his face rubbing her chest. "She's going to win a bazillion dollars."

And what were the chances of her being the last one standing and winning the prize?

"I want my mommy."

"I know, sweetie." She searched for the right words to help him. It was the first time he'd been away from Jess, and she'd apparently surprised Riley as much as Maureen. "Did she tell you she's going to be on television? On *True Grit*? Do you watch *True Grit*?"

"Yeah, with Mommy. It's kinda weird."

She would have to take his word for it, since she'd never seen an episode. But it had become a pop-culture icon, and she knew enough about it to wonder if Jess could compete. Was she strong enough, physically and mentally, to withstand the intense challenges?

"Won't it be fun to see Mommy on TV?"

"I guess."

"And *I'm* happy because I get you all to myself." What was she going to do with him? She couldn't stay home from work. And what about her vacation with Ted? He wasn't going to understand. Oh, no, he wasn't going to understand at all.

"Are you hungry? Would you like some of my super-duper chocolate-chip waffles?"

"Can I have maple syrup, too?"

Maureen refrained from shuddering at the double dose of sweetness. "Of course you can." Her mind was whirling. Why hadn't Jess left Riley with Daniel? It made no sense to bring Riley all the way down here, to take him from the only home he'd known.

But he's mine. Happiness overshadowed her questions. For just a little while she would enjoy the gift Jess had given her.

"SOMEONE'S HERE," Riley said, standing at Maureen's front window.

"A tall man with short gray hair?"

"Yeah. He's skinny."

Maureen preferred to think of Ted as lanky. He was fifty, eleven years older than she, and very handsome, turning heads everywhere they went. "That's Ted. He's my boyfriend," she said, getting up off the floor and heading toward the hallway.

"You have a boyfriend?" he asked, as if shocked.

Yeah. A stunner, isn't it? She laughed quietly as she went to the front door, opening it before Ted could knock. "Hi."

He was nine inches taller than her five foot six, so he had to stoop a little to kiss her, even as she went up on tiptoe. She moved in for a hug, more for herself than him. She dreaded telling him—

"You must be Riley," Ted said, stepping back and looking over Maureen's shoulder.

She turned. Her grandson was peeking around the doorway. "I'm Riley Joshua Cregg," he said.

"Ted Montague. Good to meet you." They shook hands like gentlemen, which made Maureen smile.

They all moved into the living room. Ted stopped and stared. "You opened a toy store."

Not exactly, but she'd dug out Jess's old toys, and Riley had brought a lot with him. They were scattered and piled throughout the room. "We couldn't decide what we wanted to play with."

"I see." He looked around. "And your daughter?"

Without comment, Maureen picked up the envelope and passed it to Ted. Halfway through reading Jess's letter, he sat in the overstuffed chair he'd claimed as his over the past few months. She looked around the room as he poured through the documents. The place really was a mess, and she generally hated mess, but she didn't mind this one, the scattering of toys and the noise of one small boy.

Her furnishings suited the Italianate Victorian facade of the building, with its pretty blue-with-white trim. The eleven-foot ceilings made the house seem bigger than its actual square footage. It was roomy enough for her—two bedrooms, a full basement with lots of storage space, a bright, cozy kitchen and big, sunny backyard. She'd bought it fifteen years ago, before the area had started to gentrify, and it was now worth a small fortune, at least to her.

Ted folded up the papers and slid them back into the envelope. He met her gaze. She'd never seen him angry before. Annoyed, maybe, but not truly angry—until now. His whole face frowned, making him look his age, when he usually looked younger.

"We'll talk about it later, okay?" she said, angling her

head toward where Riley was vrooming cars across the hardwood floor.

"Six weeks, Maureen? *Six weeks?*"

Riley looked up, responding to the strident tone by shrinking back. He shifted his gaze to Maureen, his eyes wide. She smiled and joined him on the floor, choosing a bulldozer from his construction zone and using it as if pushing a pile of dirt.

"Riley and I packed a picnic," she said. "We thought we could go to Holly Park." She felt a little guilty about telling Ted in front of Riley, since Ted would look like the bad guy if he said no.

He gave her a look that said he knew what she was doing. "Fine."

They took advantage of the nice day to walk the less-than-half-mile trek to the park. Ted held her hand but said nothing. Riley didn't hold her hand and talked nonstop. He pointed out houses, cars and dogs that caught his eye, stopping in his tracks and saying things like, "Look at that!" or "Isn't that funny?" with open exuberance and wonder. Had Jess been like that? Surely she must have been, but Maureen couldn't remember specifically.

They reached the green dome of Holly Park with its view above the rooftops. The marine layer was burning off, leaving a beautiful panorama of the city. Maureen had been to Holly Park only one other time—Jess and Riley's last visit, a year ago. The recently renovated park that used to be a blight was now an urban paradise for families.

Riley wanted Maureen to stay close as he hopped from the playhouse to the slide, then onto the swings and cargo ropes. When he got to a stretch-rope merry-go-round, he watched the other children play but didn't make a move to join them.

Even at six, he's a loner, Maureen thought, watching him. Or maybe he needed to know the lay of the land before he threw himself into the fray—which was a smart move and the opposite of his mother, who had rarely thought through anything before taking action.

Maureen gave Riley a push on a swing then glanced to where Ted sat at one of the picnic tables, staring into space. He'd been married at thirty, divorced at forty and was child-less—a conscious choice. He didn't think the city was a good place to raise children, and he was a city man through and through. His ex-wife had at first been in agreement, then changed her mind and wanted a family, after all. She divorced him, remarried and now had four children—and lived in the city. He'd kept no photos of her, not even of their wedding, so Maureen had never seen what the woman looked like.

"Higher, Grandma! Push me higher!"

He giggled as she pushed him, and she saw Ted smile at the joyful sound.

Together they ate their lunch of turkey sandwiches, chips and cookies, all things Riley had selected at the deli section at the local market. He swung his legs while he devoured his lunch, the toes of his sneakers dragging the ground, his focus on the children playing. She wished she knew him well enough to read his expression. Was he tired? Or sad, perhaps? He looked solemn, anyway, had lost his former playfulness.

"Won't be too long before you're in first grade," Maureen said.

"Grandma." His tone was tolerant. "I'm already in first grade. I graduated, you know."

"Do you like school?" Ted asked.

"It's fun. But Cody says first grade is hecka hard."

"Who's Cody?"

"He lives next door. He's seven." He took a big bite of cookie. "He knows everything."

They left the park soon after with a promise to return the next day. Riley skipped a little ahead of Maureen and Ted, stopping often to inspect items of interest. He would be ready for a nap, then Maureen would have to face the music with Ted.

"Can I have another cookie, plea— Papa!" Riley shouted as they neared the house. He took off running. "Papa!"

A man rose from his perch on Maureen's tiny porch. She'd recognize him anywhere—Daniel Cregg, Riley's paternal grandfather. Maureen's nemesis.

The man who'd stolen her daughter and grandson.

CHAPTER 3

Rileyism #1: "*I'm six. You know what that means,
don't you?*"

"Papa!" Riley opened the gate and raced up the stairs into
Daniel's arms. Envy swamped Maureen. She'd gotten a hug
from Riley only by taking one, yet he threw himself at Daniel.

Riley even had a nickname for him, Papa, while she was
just plain Grandma.

"The grandfather, I presume," Ted said as they reached
the wrought-iron gate.

"In the flesh." And she certainly couldn't fault the flesh.
He wasn't quite six feet tall, had a runner's lean build with
a weight lifter's shoulders. His dark-blond hair was thick and
wavy, not quite long enough to band into a ponytail. He
dressed like the college students he taught, in jeans, T-shirt
and a Cascade University sweatshirt, even though he was,
like Ted, fifty years old.

And he was a vegetarian. And never on time for
anything. And disorganized. All the things she disliked. But

mostly she disliked—hated—that he'd enticed her daughter and grandson away from her.

He stood on the porch nuzzling Riley into giggles as Maureen and Ted climbed the stairs.

"Hey," he said, his tone friendly.

"Doesn't anyone have the courtesy to call ahead anymore?" she asked, walking past him and unlocking her front door. "You don't own a telephone, Daniel?"

"I didn't have time to waste or the inclination to warn her that I was coming. I knew I couldn't stop her by talking to her on the phone." He set Riley down and picked up a small, scuffed, black leather bag.

Riley raced down the hallway and into the living room, his energy back in full measure. "Come see my city, Papa!"

"Just a sec, bud." Daniel extended a hand to Ted. "Daniel Cregg."

"Ted Montague."

"Oh, yeah, the boyfriend. You got yourself a…an interesting woman there." He flashed a grin at Maureen. "So, where's Jess?"

"Gone."

He paled. "Gone? She doesn't have to report until Tuesday." Gone, too, was the devil-may-care smile. "She's already in L.A.?"

Maureen glanced at her watch. "I would say she's there by now, yes. We'll talk about it while Riley's having his nap." She'd always made an effort to be civil to Daniel in front of Riley. And for the first time, she had possession, therefore control. She liked it—a lot. "Can I get you some refreshment?" she asked.

"I don't suppose you have any carrot juice?"

"Gee, Daniel, if only I'd known you were coming...." She gestured toward the sidewalk. "I can give you directions to the local health food store. You can jog there and back in twenty minutes, I would guess. Or will that interfere with your getting to the airport on time for your return flight?"

His amber eyes glittered. "Water will be fine. Thank you."

"Is tap okay?" Oh, yeah, she was enjoying herself.

"If that's all you have."

"Come in, then. I'm surprised you don't have your own with you. I can't remember seeing you without a bottle of water with that funny-looking filter on it." She headed for the kitchen, leaving Daniel in the living room. Ted followed her.

"What's going on between you two?" he asked, setting their picnic cooler on the counter.

"I told you before that we've never gotten along."

"I know you feel he's kept Jess and Riley from you all these years, but you were the one she left her son with this time. Obviously, things aren't as rosy as you thought with that relationship."

Obviously. But why? What had happened? She poured a glass of tepid tap water. "I don't *feel* he kept them from me. I *know* he did. He offered her an apartment of her own above his garage—a really nice one. He pays all of her expenses. She doesn't have any responsibilities whatsoever. Is that any way to help a teenage mother mature and become independent, as she should have been by now? Daniel hasn't helped Jess. He's enabled her. He's stunted her. And it looks like it's come back to bite him, doesn't it?"

"I think you need the full story before you decide that. Maureen, I have to say, this is a side of you I haven't seen before. It's not attractive."

Okay, maybe her smugness over Jess leaving Riley with her wasn't attractive, but she had a right to feel happy about whatever it was that had brought Riley to her after hurtful years of having so little contact. They would have a chance to have a real grandmother/grandson relationship. It was what she'd wanted for so long.

"You don't understand," she said to Ted. "You haven't had a child turn her back on you when she should've been needing you more than anyone else."

"You're right. I don't understand the situation in that particular way. But that was then, Maureen. This is now."

"And *now* is a second chance. Don't take the joy out of it. Please."

He stared at her for several long seconds, then he wrapped her in his arms and held her tight. "Okay, sweetheart," he said, resting his chin on her head. "As long as you're putting Riley's needs first."

Of course Riley's needs would take center stage, but her needs mattered, too, this time.

When they returned to the living room, Daniel was

stretched out on his stomach on the floor playing demolition derby with Riley. They were making all sorts of crash sounds—brakes squealing, metal hitting metal. Cars were flying into the air then crashing down.

Riley climbed onto Daniel's back and ran a car up his spine and into his hair, where it just about got lost in the denseness, then did get stuck.

"Oops," Riley said, tugging at the car. "Sorry, Papa."

"Ouch. Hold on, bud. You're gonna give me a bald spot."

Maureen watched Daniel try to extricate the car before she finally set down his glass of water and went up to him. "Here. Let me. Sit on the chair."

It was like performing microsurgery, unwrapping long strands of hair from the tiny tire axles, almost one by one. His hair was incredibly soft, and up close like this, she could see it was shot with silver here and there, not easily visible since his hair wasn't very dark. He bounced Riley on his knee, and they kept their heads together, as if they were telling secrets.

Maureen yanked the final few strands free to get the job over and done with.

"Hey!" He rubbed his head.

"Sorry. It wouldn't come loose."

He gave her a look of disbelief but muttered his thanks.

"Nap time," she said to Riley.

He gave her a look. "I'm six. You know what that means, don't you?"

"What does it mean?"

"I don't take naps anymore."

"A rest, then. You got up early and you played hard at the park. Just close your eyes for a little while."

"But—"

"Do as your grandmother says," Daniel said.

Which really ticked Maureen off. How dare he stick his nose where it didn't belong? But Riley had already headed for the bedroom.

"Bathroom first," Maureen said.

The three adults stood waiting, the silence awkward. When Riley emerged she followed him into the bedroom and made sure he took off his sneakers before getting onto the bed. She handed Stripe to him, then covered him with an afghan that Cherie had crocheted and kissed his forehead.

"I'm not gonna sleep," he said, the words muffled by the stuffed tiger.

"That's fine."

"Papa will still be here when I get up, won't he?"

"I don't know what his plans are. But I'm sure he'll say goodbye before he goes anywhere." *Like back to Seattle on the next available flight.*

"You promise?"

"I promise."

"Okay." He pulled the afghan up to his chin then. "Don't shut the door."

"I won't shut it all the way."

When she returned to the living room, she found Ted in

her big chair and Daniel picking up the toys, putting them in their plastic containers.

"Thanks," she said.

"He likes to start over. There's something about creating a new city that appeals to him."

"Maybe he'll be a builder," she said, taking a seat on the sofa, next to Ted's chair. She was determined to stay calm.

"Maybe." Daniel picked up his glass of water and sat down, too. He looked at Ted. "I don't think I heard what you do for a living."

"I'm a CPA and financial planner."

"How did you two meet?"

"At work," Maureen said. "I'm not sure if Jess told you about Carlos Martinez, my boss at Primero Publishing? He passed away suddenly five months ago, and his wife, Bernadette, stepped in as publisher. Ted's been a friend of theirs for years. She asked him to take a look at the company finances."

"Then I took a look at Maureen, too," he said, smiling at her.

She smiled back. "He came along at a busy time, since we'd just started working on two new projects a couple of months before Carlos died. We're trying to see them through, but it's taking everything out of us."

"She works very long hours," Ted said, laying a hand on her shoulder, his fingers resting against her collarbone in a proprietary way, making Maureen uncomfortable. She'd never seen him possessive.

"It took me months," he went on, "but I finally convinced her to take a vacation. We're leaving two weeks from today."

The implications of that statement reverberated through the room. They all knew Jess was supposed to be gone for six weeks.

Maureen was stuck. She needed to tell Ted that they would have to postpone their vacation, but she couldn't do it in front of Daniel.

"Why are you here?" she asked Daniel, taking control of the discussion. "What did you hope to accomplish by just showing up?"

He dragged his hands down his face. "We had an argument."

"You and Jess? About what?"

"About this harebrained scheme of hers to be on *True Grit*."

Maureen might have agreed with him, but she wasn't going to let him criticize her daughter. "My understanding is that she beat almost impossible odds to make it onto the program." She and Riley had looked it up on the Internet that morning. "So many people apply, yet she was chosen. It's a huge accomplishment."

"I'm not denying that. I even had a hand in it, since I'm the one that got her training. She's become quite an athlete."

"I could tell. When I hugged her, I could tell. I would think you would be proud she got on the show."

"Proud? What about her job?"

"She had a job?"

"You didn't know?"

Maureen shook her head. "She never said. What was she doing?"

"She's an assistant in my department at the university."

"Since when?"

"Since Riley started kindergarten last year. She only works—worked—part-time, just while he's in school. It was ideal. She would've been able to increase her hours as his school days got longer."

"Would have?"

He nodded. "She's supposed to be there now, for summer session. She quit."

Why hadn't Jess told her? How little she knew of her daughter's life.

"So, you arranged the job for her?"

"Yeah. I stuck my neck out, too, since she didn't have any experience, and there were other candidates more qualified. I thought it might get her interested in going to college. Her tuition would've been almost free." He tunneled his fingers through his hair.

That soft, thick— Maureen caught herself. "She's lived with you all these years and you don't know what a dreamer Jess is?" she asked, not unkindly. "This is the big-fantasy kind of thing that Jess thrives on."

Daniel leaned his arms on his thighs and turned his head to look at her. "I didn't think she'd go through with it, in the end. She may be a dreamer, but she usually has little follow-through. I certainly never expected her to take off as she did. I was out of town. She left me a note."

"And you hopped a plane without calling first? What if Jess hadn't come here? What if I hadn't been home?"

He frowned. "Where would you be? You're always home."

She really needed to get away more.

"Anyway," Daniel went on, "Jess said in her note she was leaving Riley here, but I knew you probably couldn't take much time off from work, and I'm off for the summer…."

"This works out perfectly," Ted said, participating in the conversation for the first time. "We can figure out a way to keep the boy until we go on vacation, then he can go back to you for the remainder of the time."

Daniel cheered up. "I could work with that—"

"No." Maureen didn't raise her voice. Her heart pounded in her ears. She could barely swallow. She felt both men focus on her, and for a moment she looked out the front window, not wanting to continue what was bound to be a hard conversation.

"No?" Ted repeated, shock in his tone. "Maureen, it's the perfect solution. And obviously the boy loves being with his grandfather."

Yes, he does. Way too much. "Jess left him with *me*. I'm sure she had her reasons."

"Now, hold on a minute," Daniel said. "Jess and I had an argument. She's not used to being denied anything, and so she decided to get back at me by bringing Riley here. It's not as if she doesn't trust me with him."

"How do I know that? The only thing I know for sure is that she wanted me to have Riley for the time she's gone. The whole time. Period."

"We need to talk about this," Ted said with a telling glance at Daniel.

Daniel, obviously realizing that Ted was his ally in his cause, offered to go for a walk.

"Don't you have a plane to catch or something?" Maureen asked, annoyed that the men were ganging up on her.

"I bought a one-way ticket."

"Of course you did," she muttered. "Fine. Go for a walk. Or go into my backyard." Or go to hell.

He stood. "How much time should I give you?"

"Fifteen minutes?" Ted said when Maureen clammed up. "If you turn right when you leave the house and walk a few blocks, you'll hit Cortland Avenue. That's the commercial district. You'll find a couple of places to get something to eat, if you want."

"Thanks." Then he was gone, and the air was filled with unspoken accusations.

Maureen didn't trust herself to say the right thing. Angry, she pushed herself up and went to the front window, spotting Daniel as he made his way up the street, that jaunty walk of his annoying her even more.

"I don't appreciate your interference," she said to Ted, her back to him.

"Interference? This situation involves me, too. Why shouldn't I be allowed my opinions?"

"Opinions are one thing. Decisions without discussion are another."

"What do you mean?"

She faced him, crossed her arms. "You decided what would happen. I wasn't given a say in the matter." And it made her look weak in Daniel's eyes, she thought. She couldn't afford any sign of weakness or Daniel would pounce on it in some way, maybe even enlist Riley in his cause. Riley would probably like nothing better than to go back with Daniel. That thought hurt. "Your plan isn't going to work for me, Ted."

"Meaning what?"

"Meaning we need to postpone the vacation."

Silence descended, deafening and tense.

He came close to her. "Postponing is the same as canceling, and you know it. It took me weeks to convince you to take this trip. If anything happens to interfere with it, we'll never go."

"Even without Riley it's a horrible time for me to be gone, and you know *that*. Everything at work is tenuous. I've got a shot to be vice president. If I leave, I could very well be saying goodbye to that opportunity."

"Bernadette gave her enthusiastic approval for you to go."

"What else could she say? You're not there every day, under the gun. I know what's going on, and I know it's going to be hard for them without me."

"You're not indispensable. And it's only two weeks."

She heard the underlying anger in his voice, his frustration with her. She understood it, but it didn't change the fact she had the opportunity to really connect with her grandson for the first time—and by default, reconnect with her daughter. To Maureen, it wasn't even a decision.

"A postponement, Ted. That's all. I need to do this. I need to have this time with Riley. And Jess *did* leave him with me. She certainly wouldn't want me to pawn him off on someone else. I'm sorry. I know it's horrible of me to ask you to change plans on such short notice, but I can't do anything else. I need you to understand that."

His whole body seemed to sigh. "We'll probably have penalties to pay for changing our reservations—if we can even get changes. That'll put us into August. You do realize that Europe goes on vacation in August, right? It could change a lot of our plans."

"The Louvre will still be there, right? And the Eiffel Tower?" She slipped her arms around him. "And the Venice canals? The Tower of London?"

"I get your point." He kissed her, but not with much depth or warmth. "I spent a lot of time researching the right hotels and the most efficient train schedules and the best restaurants."

"We'll find a bed to sleep in and trains to ride and places to eat." She wasn't going to back down, so she hoped that *he* would. If he didn't, she didn't know what she would do.

She remembered his excitement when he gave her his house key. Was she willing to give up all that it represented for this brief time with Riley? She'd been alone all her adult life, having a few relationships that never got anywhere near marriage and having a permanent partner for the rest of her life. Ted was a real possibility for that changing. But if she had to make a choice… There *was* no choice.

"All right," Ted said after a long, tense silence. "I'll re-arrange the trip. Jess will be back toward the end of July, right? We'll allow an extra week, in case something else comes up. We'll leave on your birthday, August fourth. Okay?"

Her fortieth. She would be celebrating a new beginning to her life as she marked that auspicious birthday—a new relationship with her daughter and grandson, a solid, steady relationship with a man and, hopefully, a new job with loads of responsibility and a nice pay raise.

Turning forty looked to be a banner year.

"Thank you, Ted," she said, relaxing against him. "I can't tell you how much this means to me."

"Sweetheart, I see how much it means or I wouldn't be doing it. Just don't let it take over your life completely, okay? I need attention, too."

He was right about that. He'd been so patient about her long work weeks that left her exhausted and edgy. "I'll try to do better," she said. "I don't mean to ignore you."

"I know you don't." He released her. "You're going to need a sitter or day care or something."

"Yes. I'll get busy on that."

"What're you going to do about Daniel?"

"Tell him to enjoy his cab ride back to the airport."

"Something tells me it's not going to be that easy."

"He doesn't really have a choice, does he?"

He shrugged. "Do you need me to stay until he's gone? I'd like to get going on the changes in our itinerary."

"That's fine. I can deal with Daniel alone." Preferred to. She was glad Ted didn't care whether or not he was there. "And Riley will want to spend a little time with him. I can't send him away until they've had a chance to talk."

She walked him to the door and kissed him goodbye, all the while hoping Daniel would get back before Riley woke up. She couldn't have the honest conversation she needed to have with Daniel in front of Riley, but have it she would.

Really, Daniel had some nerve. All these years he'd had the upper hand. It was her turn.

And there was no way she was going to give an inch to him. No way at all.

CHAPTER 4

Rileyism #2: "I don't want to be rotten."

"Grandma, I'm hungry."

Maureen looked sharply at her watch. Where was Daniel? He'd been gone for three hours. No call. Nothing. "How about some grapes?" she said.

"How about some cookies?" he asked with that missing-tooth smile.

She couldn't help but smile back. "Too close to dinner."

"Aw, man."

She patted the gelled spikes on his head. "Grapes, then?"

"I guess. How come Papa's not back yet?"

Because Papa is an inconsiderate jerk. "He must be enjoying seeing San Francisco," she said instead.

The front door burst open then, and Daniel breezed in as if he were welcome.

"Hey, bud," he said, crouching down as Riley ran to him. "How was the nap?"

"I rested, Papa. I didn't nap."

Right. He didn't nap for two whole hours, Maureen

thought with a smile. He'd been so soundly asleep that he hadn't even flinched when she'd checked on him and had bumped into a chair that skittered a few inches across the hardwood floor.

Daniel looked up at Maureen. His hair was wind-tossed, his face surprisingly tanned for a man who lived in rainy Seattle. He looked years younger than the fifty he was.

"What's the verdict?" he asked, standing. Riley looked at Maureen, too, as he leaned against his grandfather's legs, Daniel's hands on his shoulders. The two Cregg men made an indomitable force.

Where have you been all this time? "We're going to do what Jess asked."

"Okay."

Okay? *O-kay?* Now what game was he playing, to give in without a fight? "I'm glad you agree," she said, aware of how still Riley was, and how he'd reached up with both hands to grab Daniel's.

"Didn't say I agree, but I understand your position."

"Do you need a ride to the airport?" She figured that was the least she could do.

"No, thanks. In fact, I'm not going anywhere for, oh, I figure about six weeks."

"What?" She plunked her fists on her hips.

"I found myself a place to live—one of the kids who works at the health food store offered his spare bedroom. Seems his roommate is gone for the summer, so he's in need of the cash."

"Why would you do that?"

"I've never been to San Francisco. I'm off for the summer. And I figure you need someone to watch Riley during the day while you work. I'm your man."

All the things Maureen wanted to say stuck in her throat when she saw how happy Riley was. The arrogant Daniel Cregg. He'd given her no choice. He'd set his course without discussing it with her, then presented it to her in front of Riley. If she told Daniel he wasn't welcome, she would be the bad guy. Then what chance would she have of forging a new bond with Riley, one she hoped would seal things between them for life?

"I already have day care lined up," she said tightly.

"Hey, I'm free—in both senses of the word. It's a win-win situation. There's a lot to see and do in this city. Riley and I will explore. It'll be fun, and educational."

"I have plans to show him things, too, you know."

"Look, Maureen, which do you want? Day care, where he sits around and plays video games and watches television? Or an adventure every day—fresh air and new experiences? You'll have him every night and every weekend, the same as you would if I weren't here. There's plenty of time for both of us."

She didn't know how much Riley was understanding of their conversation, but he seemed anxious.

"What kind of apartment will you be living in?"

"The kind college kids can afford. Two small bedrooms, a kitchen sink piled with dirty dishes. Pizza boxes jammed into overflowing trash cans."

"And the kid works in a health-food store?"

"I'm sure they were vegetarian pizzas."

She refused to smile at that. "It doesn't sound like a healthy environment to me." For Riley, she added mentally, assuming Daniel would pick up on that.

"We'll use your house as our home base, if that's okay with you. You walk in the door at night, I walk out."

Like she really had a choice? She couldn't stop him from renting a room. She couldn't keep him away from Riley without being the mean ol' grandma. And having Daniel instead of some stranger care for Riley was a good thing.

"Do you have to go back to Seattle and pick up clothes and whatever?"

"Nope. I asked a friend to pack up my whatevers, including my laptop, and airfreight them. So, how about I take you two to dinner, then I'll show you where I'll be living."

She should call Ted and let him know what was happening, but decided to wait until after Riley went to bed, so she could have a private conversation. She didn't know whether the new plan would make Ted happy or not. He'd seemed not to like Daniel very much—until Daniel had become a solution to a problem that directly affected Ted.

"Dinner sounds good to me," she said finally. "As long as the restaurant serves normal food. And meat."

"What's normal?" He grinned. "I don't force my convictions on others, Mo."

"Don't call me that. Please," she added, softening the order for Riley's sake. Daniel's calling her Mo reminded her of her father, and he was the last person she wanted to be reminded of. Well, him and Jess's father. "Would you mind if I ask my aunt to join us? She hasn't seen Riley since last year." And Ted couldn't get irritated with another adult along.

"Sure. I've never met the old gal. Do we need to pick her up?"

"She'll walk. She doesn't live far from Cortland. And she wouldn't appreciate you calling her 'the old gal.' You remember Auntie Cherie, don't you, Riley?"

He nodded several times. "She's fun."

"Exactly. Let me give her a call and see if she's free. The woman has a busy calendar." Maureen went into her bedroom and shut the door. She leaned against it for a few seconds, forcing herself to relax. It wasn't a matter of coming out the winner over Daniel, although that was a nice side benefit, but of her not backing down from what she wanted. She'd stood up for herself. She didn't consider herself a weak woman, but, with the exception of at her job, she tended to go along with what anyone else wanted to do, in order to keep peace. She liked peace. She liked order. The one time she hadn't been the model of responsibility had resulted in her becoming pregnant and a single mother at seventeen.

But this time the stakes were too high to give in to Ted *or* Daniel. She needed Riley and Jess in her life. So, she'd stood up for herself.

And it felt pretty darn good.

MAUREEN SAW RILEY spot Cherie coming into the Peace-Love Café. He was kneeling on a chair at the table and started waving both arms to get her attention. They had seen each other several times through the years, and occasionally Cherie would talk with him over the computer camera. Now Riley would have a chance to really get to know her well, too. *Thank you, Jess.*

"There you are!" Cherie called, waving off the hostess, then heading toward them. She greeted at least a half-dozen guests as she made her way through the funky restaurant, a throwback to the old flower-power days complete with psychedelic art on the walls and the servers wearing beads, headbands and long, flowing outfits.

Daniel stood and held a chair for Cherie, but first she went around the table, giving hugs and kisses. She included Daniel before she sat down, as if they were old friends.

"You don't quite fit the picture I had of you in my head," she said to Daniel after ordering a glass of white zinfandel.

"Which was?"

"I was thinking, Dr. Cregg, professor of English. Tweed jackets and a pipe. A bow tie, maybe, receding hair line. And a certain tone."

"What kind of tone?"

"A sort of lofty use of language, with a Bostonian accent, even if he came from Baton Rouge."

He laughed. "I've met those professors. They were my inspirations to be the opposite."

"A worthy goal." She leaned toward Maureen. "So, adorable girl, what's going on?"

Maureen summed up the events in an upbeat manner as Riley used the restaurant-supplied crayons to draw on their butcher-paper tablecloth.

"Will you take me to the 'ramics place, Auntie Cherie? I want to make my mom an I-Love-You plate for when she comes back to get me," he said, lifting his head finally.

"That's a date, young man."

His smile lit up his entire face and got even wider somehow when she picked up a crayon and started drawing with him. Forehead to forehead, they chattered like old friends.

Daniel was uncharacteristically quiet.

"You must be tired," Maureen said to him.

"Huh? Oh, yeah. A little. How is it you can get jet lag without leaving the time zone?"

"It's just your body letting down from the stress of travel," Cherie said. "A good night's sleep and you'll be right as rain."

"I wonder how good my nights are going to be," he said. "My new roomie, Ty, gets off work at nine. I think his night is just beginning at that point. Should be interesting. Think I'll be bunkin' with you, Master Riley, when you na—rest in the afternoon."

Riley frowned. "Grandma doesn't have bunk beds, Papa."

Daniel grinned. "It's an expression, bud. It means lying down to rest."

"Maybe you'd like to help me one day when I deliver meals," Cherie said.

"Do you have a motorcycle? Our pizza guy has a motorcycle."

"Wouldn't that be fun? Alas, I don't even have a driver's license, so they give me a driver. He waits in the car while I take the dinners inside to people who can't fix a meal for themselves."

"Why can't they?" He'd abandoned his artwork to listen to her.

"Mostly because they're old. Like me."

He giggled. "You're not *old*."

"Well. Isn't that nice?" She beamed. "Do you think you'd like to help me out sometime? Your grandma helps on Saturdays. They'd love to see that sweet smile of yours, I can tell you that."

"Sure. I can, can't I, Papa?"

Maureen took a quick swig of her wine, hiding her hurt that Riley had asked Daniel for permission instead of her. He was staying with *her*.

"That's up to your grandma," Daniel said. "She's the boss now."

"Can I, Grandma?"

"Of course." She caught Cherie looking intently at her.

"I hafta go to the bathroom."

"Okay, bud." Daniel stood. "Let's go."

"What's got your knickers in a twist?" Cherie asked the second they were alone.

"I wish Daniel weren't here. Frankly, I want Riley to myself."

"Well, *I* can see your jealousy, Maureen, and Riley's going to pick up on that, too. You've *got* Riley. Let go of the old hurt, and everyone will be happier."

"I'm trying."

"Building a relationship takes time."

"I know." Maureen rubbed her forehead. "I do know. He calls Daniel Papa." She put a hand to her mouth. She hadn't meant to say that out loud, to sound belligerent about it.

"What's wrong with that?"

"Daniel has a nickname, Papa. Riley calls me Grandma. Nothing special."

Cherie sat back, holding her wineglass, swirling the contents. "Papa is probably the most common variation on Grandpa. It's those double-repeat syllables that babies learn so much easier—mama, dada, papa. He was there every day with Riley. Aren't you being overly sensitive?"

"Maybe." Probably. "It's just been a long, trying day dealing with everything."

Cherie sipped her wine, then set down the glass gently. "How's Ted taking it all?"

Maureen summed it up, adding, "He's being amazingly patient."

"Hmm."

"What's that supposed to mean?"

"I've been wondering how he would handle it if you ever *didn't* go along with what he wanted."

"I don't know what that means, Cherie."

"Just what I said. You defer to him, that's all. Today you didn't. I'm glad he's being patient."

Even if Maureen had wanted to explore the point further, Daniel and Riley returned then.

"Grandma, that bathroom is crazy!"

Since Maureen was a regular customer at the restaurant, she knew what Riley had discovered. "How is it crazy?"

"There's no reg'lar lights but there's colors all over the walls and they…glow. What's it called, Papa?"

"Day-Glo paint and black lights."

"Black lights. Isn't that funny? Papa says that's what the hippers liked."

"Hippies," Cherie said. She touched her peace-symbol necklace. "I was a hippie."

"You were?" His eyes went round. "Did you glow?"

Cherie laughed. "Oh, honey, did I ever. I glowed like a neon sign."

"I'll show you pictures," Maureen said. "She was beautiful."

"She's still beautiful," Daniel said, lifting his glass in a toast.

"Well. Flattery will get you everywhere." Cherie clinked glasses with him, then Riley wanted to join in. After much toasting and clinking, their meals were brought and everyone dug in as if they hadn't eaten in days.

After dinner they walked to Daniel's apartment. Ty wasn't there.

"This isn't too bad," Maureen said, looking around. Nothing was new but it wasn't too cluttered or dirty.

"I decided to clean the place up a little before I went back to your house. It reminded me too much of dorm life." Daniel led them into his bedroom. He turned to Maureen. "Any chance you've got an extra set of sheets you can loan me? I don't think even bleach will help these." He lifted the ratty quilt to unearth equally ratty sheets.

Maureen pictured his house in Seattle, a three-bedroom craftsman with wood-shingle siding on a quiet, tree-lined street, a far cry from this tiny, street-noisy place. She caught Cherie's pointed look.

"I'd be glad to loan you some bedding," Maureen said. "Anything else you need?"

"Nope, thanks."

Cherie glanced at her watch. "I'm supposed to meet some friends in a few minutes, so I'll leave you. Thank you for dinner, Daniel." She hugged Riley. "We'll make a date soon, okay?"

"Okay. Auntie Cherie? You know my mom, right?"

"I know your mom very well. Your mom and grandma lived with me until your mom was six, just like you."

"Really?"

"That's right."

"She'll come back, right?" he said, almost whispering.

Maureen's throat ached. Why did he have so little faith in his mother returning? Why was he so insecure? Jess had never once left him.

"She'll be back just as soon as she's done with the TV show."

"You promise?"

"I promise." Cherie looked at Maureen then Daniel. "In the meantime, you've got two doting grandparents and one doting great-aunt to spoil you rotten."

"I don't want to be rotten. I—"

"It's an expression," Daniel interrupted. "It's an okay thing, bud. She means you're going to have a whole lot of fun."

"Oh. Okay." He grinned finally.

"May I escort you where you're headed?" Daniel asked Cherie.

"Wouldn't that shock and delight my girlfriends, me walking into the club with a young stud on my arm." She laughed. "Maybe another time. But thanks."

They all left the apartment, Cherie heading in the opposite direction. Back at her house, Maureen loaded bedding and a fresh pillow into a shopping bag and brought it to Daniel where he was sitting with Riley, playing Go Fish.

"I added a can of air freshener," she said.

Daniel grinned, and for the first time Maureen saw Riley in him. She'd never noticed before, maybe because she and Daniel hadn't smiled at each other much.

"It did have a hint of unwashed student about it, didn't it?" Daniel said.

"More than a hint."

"All part of the adventure. Go Fish," he said to Riley.

Maureen sat next to her grandson but addressed Daniel. "This is an adventure to you?"

"Isn't it? Something unexpected. A chance to explore a part of the country I never have before—and not just for a weekend but for enough time to really get to know a place."

"Is there a girlfriend at home who's not too happy about this?" Almost instantly she folded her hands in her lap and tried not to fidget. She didn't know how to take the nosy question back.

"Do you have any sixes, bud?" His eyes sparkled at her discomfort. "Not one in particular."

"Go Fish. Papa has lots of girlfriends," Riley said matter of factly. "Do you have any Ks?"

"What are Ks?"

"Kings?"

"Right. Yep. Here you go."

Papa has lots of girlfriends. He'd played a wide field for as long as she'd known him, never committing to any one woman, and most of them substantially younger. She studied him now, playing the card game animatedly with Riley, making him giggle. She wondered what he was like in the classroom. It was hard to picture him in the role of English professor, as Cherie had pointed out. He didn't fit any stereotypical mold. She bet his students loved him—

"You beat me again," Daniel said, ruffling Riley's hair, most of the gel having worn off during the course of the day. "I'll hit the road." He stood.

Riley threw himself against him. "I don't want you to leave."

"Hey, bud. You saw where I'm living. I won't be far away."

"Sleep in my bed. You'll fit."

A part of Maureen understood Riley's fear. A different part was hurt that Riley didn't want to be alone with her. It wasn't as if they were strangers, after all.

"I'll be seeing you lots. So much that you'll get sick of me and wish I'd go away." Daniel lifted him and rocked him side to side, Riley's legs dangling and flying, making him giggle again. "You sleep tight."

"Don't let the bedbugs bite," Riley finished. "Will you be here when I wake up in the morning?"

"I will. Or before your grandma heads out, anyway."

Maureen followed him down the hall to the front door. "Thank you, Daniel."

"No reason why we can't work together on this. Give him some great memories."

"I agree."

"I know you hate me," he said. "But this can be our chance for a new start, too. For Riley's and Jess's sake. And our own."

"I don't hate you."

He lifted his brows.

"I resent you," she said, then added, "with reason."

"That sounds so much better."

"And I've been really pissed off at you. And stuck pins in a voodoo doll that happens to look like you." She smiled, taking the edge off the words.

"And if that doesn't add up to hate…"

"I can see where you might think that."

He grinned. "Your aunt's quite a woman."

"She is, indeed. I don't know where I would be today without her."

"I'd like to hear more about that sometime."

"I'd like to tell you. Sometime."

"Good night, Maureen. Sweet dreams."

He walked away, and Maureen went off to tuck her sweet grandson in bed. How much had changed in just a day—Riley was hers for now, and Daniel? Well, there might be more to him than she'd thought. Time would tell.

But for now life didn't get much better than this.

CHAPTER 5

Rileyism #3: "I have everything under control."

The following morning Maureen paced her living room in front of the window. Back and forth, stop to look outside, back and forth again. Why hadn't she asked for Daniel's cell phone number? He was always late. She should've told him fifteen minutes earlier than she actually needed him to arrive. If she was late to work because of him…

She spotted him jogging up the street and hurried to the front door to fling it open.

"Good morning," he said, as if nothing were wrong.

"You're late."

He merely raised his brows.

His hair was wet, either from a shower or the jog, which might have started an hour ago, for all she knew. He was annoyingly faithful about anything related to physical fitness, but not about everything else in life.

"I'm going to be late to work," she said, arms crossed.

"You look…official," he said of her gray pantsuit and crisp white blouse.

She didn't think he was complimenting her. He wore not-new shorts he must've packed in his carry-on bag, and a Golden Gate Bridge T-shirt he must've bought since his arrival.

"If this is going to work for us, Daniel, you need to be on time. I don't like starting my day frazzled."

"Yes, ma'am," he said, succeeding in making her feel like a shrew, when all she wanted was to catch her bus at the normal time and get to work at her normal time. The distance between Bernal Heights, where she lived, and the Mission District, where she worked, was short, but too far to walk in less than fifteen minutes.

"How'd you sleep?" she asked, forcing the harsh edge off her tone as they walked down her hallway, aware that Riley was within hearing range.

"Dead to the world." He held up the shopping bag she'd sent him home with the night before. "Mind if I use your washer? My stuff could be delivered this afternoon, but maybe not until tomorrow."

"Be my guest." She passed him a business card. "Here's my work information. Please call if you have any questions."

Riley pounced on him then and she was off to work. She did miss her usual bus, but still arrived at work just at eight o'clock. She didn't stop to chitchat with her coworkers, instead heading straight to her boss's office. It was empty, a rarity. Maureen left a note on the desk, then settled into her own office. Only one voice mail awaited her—

"Hi, Mom. I just wanted to let you know that I got here okay. I hope you forgive me. I really am doing this for my son, the same way you sacrificed a lot for me. I just don't have your patience to take it year by year. I kind of want it now. I know, I know. Gee, what a surprise." Maureen could hear the smile in Jess's voice. "But you'll see. It'll be a good thing. I'll talk to you as soon as I'm allowed to. Tell Riley I love him. Bye."

The time stamp at the end of the message indicated Jess had called the day before, Sunday, apparently not willing to talk in person, probably not wanting to get an earful from Maureen. Smart girl.

Maureen might have surprised Jess, however, by not arguing with her, except to challenge her daughter about why she didn't feel she could've just asked if she could leave Riley instead of simply taking off as she did.

It was probably best for Riley, too, not talking to his mom. That way he could settle in. Maybe Jess was being responsible in that, too. If it was true that she really was pursuing this dream of hers to give herself and Riley a shot at independence and a good future, then Maureen couldn't fault her for it, just as Maureen had left Cherie's house and made her own way in the world.

The manner in which Maureen and Jess sought independence may be different, opposite really, but the goal was the same.

"Good morning, good morning." The cheerful greeting accompanied the arrival of Esperanza Ochoa, Maureen's coworker and friend, one of two full-time proofreader/editor/ researchers with the company. She breezed into Maureen's office, looking gorgeous and rested, and landed in the chair opposite Maureen's desk, a bright smile on her face.

"Same to you, sunshine."

Anza leaned closer and singsonged in a whisper, "I've got a secret."

"One you're going to tease me about or share?"

"Share. But only with you. No one else can know, okay?"

"Do you really have to ask?" Maureen could guess the secret but waited for confirmation.

"I'm pregnant. Six weeks."

Maureen flashed back to when she'd found out she was pregnant—just turned seventeen and scared to death. There'd been no happy glow on her face, like Anza's now. No ecstatic husband, which Gabe undoubtedly was.

"That's wonderful news! Congratulations," Maureen said, coming around her desk to hug her friend and feeling a sudden rush of envy. "I'm so happy for you both," she said, meaning it, but struggling past her own surprising emotions.

"Thank you." Anza's voice quavered and she hugged Maureen tighter. "It took a year, but finally I will be a mom. Finally."

They moved apart as they heard someone walking nearby.

"How was your weekend?" Anza asked.

"Eventful. Can we have lunch today? I'll tell you then."

"It's a date."

"What's a date?" Bernadette Martinez, the president and owner of Primero Publishing, strolled in. She was the most stylish woman Maureen knew, although the past five months since her husband had passed away had taken their toll. Until recently Bernadette looked ten years younger than the forty-eight she really was. But who wouldn't look worn-out after losing her husband and inheriting the job of running a rapidly expanding company?

"Anza and I were just making a lunch date," Maureen said as her friend slipped out.

Bernadette took Anza's seat and held up the piece of paper Maureen had left on her desk. "You wanted to see me?"

"I wanted to let you know I won't be going on vacation as scheduled. We're postponing until August fourth."

"Okay. How come?"

"I have inherited my grandson for the next six weeks." She turned a framed photo on her desk toward Bernadette and gave her a short version of how Riley came to stay with her. "I think you can probably appreciate that I would like to spend as much time with him as possible, and since I normally am just getting home about the time he goes to bed, that's going to be difficult. I'm wondering if I could leave work earlier, say at five, and then work at home after he goes to bed?"

No clock ticked, yet Maureen heard one in her head. The past few months had been overwhelming, since they'd taken on the projects that Carlos had started but hadn't yet completed before his death. Maureen's job as the liaison between Primero and the various writers was crucial, as she kept track of every project and author.

"That would be okay," Bernadette said finally. "As long as it's only six weeks. You're a key player, after all, plus I don't want others to think they can do the same thing."

Maureen hid her surprise. She'd been working ten-hour days since being hired nineteen years ago, and twelve-hour days for the past several months. Most of the other employees put in the same long hours. She never used up her annual sick leave, and had so much vacation carryover, she could be off for months with pay. Not that she would….

She thanked her boss and settled down to work, although not with her usual focus. Her life, which had seemed in perfect order—a steady boyfriend and being on the fast track at work for a promotion—was suddenly topsy-turvy.

It was difficult for Ted, too, she knew, although he'd called to say he'd gotten their itinerary changed, with only a small penalty and almost the same hotel arrangements, which seemed to ease his mind. She'd been reading a bedtime story to Riley and had rushed Ted through the conversation, then felt guilty about it. She would've called him back later, knowing he generally stayed up until midnight, but she'd fallen asleep on the couch, not waking up until 2:00 a.m., when she shuffled off to bed.

She hadn't talked to him this morning because he liked to sleep in, then work from home for a couple of hours before going to the office. Weekends were sometimes difficult for her because she woke up at six and he wanted to sleep until nine.

Maureen stared at the San Francisco-skyline poster on her wall and wondered what Riley and Daniel were doing.

She eyed her phone. Should she call home, even if just to say hi to Riley? She'd woken up at six to find him in bed with her, and had no idea when he'd joined her. She couldn't remember Jess ever getting into bed with her during the middle of the night. In fact, she remembered telling Jess she had to stay in her own bed, that she was a big girl.

Not her finest moment as a mom. Look what she'd missed—waking up to that warm little body huddled close, needing her.

Maureen pressed her face into her hands for a second. She'd been a rules-and-regulations kind of parent.

Just like her father.

She'd learned her lessons the hard way. The one time she'd rebelled against his rules she'd ended up pregnant. She'd toed the line ever since. Had made Jess toe the line. Not that Jess had done so.

On the contrary, Jess had kept moving the line as it suited her, rarely putting a toe to it, and ending up in exactly the same position as Maureen at the same age—pregnant and unmarried, not yet done with high school. At least her daughter had finished school. And the baby's father had wanted to marry her. If he hadn't died…

Maureen sent an e-mail to the staff explaining about Riley

and how she would be leaving at five and then working from home, so that everyone understood what was going on. She got back several nice notes, and a few people stopped in to personally tell her to enjoy her time with her grandson. Two coworkers were in line for the same promotion as she— Ginny Barber, who was in charge of payroll and accounting, and Doug Fairlane, the office manager. Both Ginny and Doug had been with Primero longer than Maureen.

And those two also seemed to give her the heartiest fare-wells when she left at five that night. Normally the staff got along exceptionally well, but now that there was a competition brewing for the vice president position, there was a tension in the air not normally in evidence. She wished Bernadette would make up her mind soon, before the cama-raderie suffered.

Maureen didn't know anyone on the five-o'clock bus, and it wasn't until she stepped off that she realized she didn't know what she would fix for dinner. When she was alone she usually heated up a frozen dinner. Who wanted to cook at eight o'clock? If Ted joined her, he picked up something on his way.

She should've shopped.

Maureen opened the door to an incredible aroma. She eyed two large suitcases with courier tags attached to the handles, then she wandered down the hall into the kitchen. Riley stood on a chair in front of the sink washing lettuce leaves, and Daniel stirred a mouthwatering mix in a large pot.

"Barefoot and cooking," she said, drawing their atten-tion. "That's the way it should be."

"Hi, Grandma," Riley said. He didn't hop down from the chair to greet her, so she walked over and hugged him. "I'm making salad."

"So, I see." She eyed the bowl on the counter, filled halfway with chopped tomatoes, cucumbers, avocado and green onions.

"I have to dry the lettuce real good so the dressing sticks."

"You're doing a great job." She looked at Daniel, wanting to set the right tone in front of Riley. "You didn't need to make dinner. But thank you."

"You're welcome. It's Riley's favorite."

"Papa's a *good* cooker."

"What is it?"

"Aubergine-and-black-bean chili," Daniel said. "And there'll be enough for leftovers for a couple of meals."

"Aubergine? It sounds…purple."

He laughed. "It's another name for eggplant."

"I see. You fancy up the name and it tastes better?"

"To the nonvegetarian, maybe. Oh, and we called your boyfriend and invited him for dinner, but we thought we'd surprise *you*. Why don't you go change, and I'll pour you a glass of wine?"

Geez, a girl could get used to this, she thought, a little dazed. She told herself she was giving in so easily to him sort of taking over her life and telling her what to do because she didn't want things uncomfortable for Riley. Was it really a lie if you only lied to yourself?

Maureen stopped just inside her bedroom door. On her

bed were a couple of small stacks of laundry, all neatly folded, including her bras and underwear. She moved closer, pictured him tucking the bra cups inside each other and folding her panties into neat little bundles. They weren't overly sexy, just beige or black, and nothing lacy or push-up, but the thought of him handling her private things and having that kind of intimate knowledge of her embarrassed her like nothing else had in a very long time.

Feeling her face heat up, she shoved the clothes into drawers and changed into jeans, a blue-striped blouse and white sneakers. She touched a finger to her tongue, then rubbed a spot of dirt off one sneaker. She was stalling, not knowing what to say to Daniel that wouldn't make her again sound like a shrew. But Riley *was* there, and she couldn't get angry at Daniel in front of him over what would be perceived as a normal household chore.

She went into the kitchen, keeping her gaze on Daniel. He turned just his head toward her, capturing her gaze, then he let his take a slow journey down and back up.

"I didn't have enough for a full load," he said, anticipating her possible tirade, she supposed. "Seemed like a waste of water and energy not to do yours at the same time."

Her full hamper had been sitting beside the washer. He couldn't have missed it.

But he could've ignored it.

"I hung your…delicates on the line out back. Figured you probably didn't put them in the dryer. Most women don't, anyway."

He was laughing at her. Oh, yes, he was having a great time at her expense.

"I don't know what to say," she said, finally finding her voice.

"Thank you?" He passed her a glass of merlot and kept his voice low. "You're welcome, Double-D. I hope you're going to invest in something a little more...lacy for the vacation."

So, he'd even looked at the tag on her bra. "Not every man needs a crutch to arouse him," she whispered, moving past him to where Riley was tearing up lettuce leaves and adding them to the salad bowl.

"Every man likes a woman who's confident enough to want to please," Daniel said. "We appreciate...effort."

"That looks like a very good salad," Maureen said to Riley. "Do you need any help?"

"I have everything under control," he said, like a little adult, which made her smile.

"But if your grandma would like to set the table," Daniel said, "that would be good."

Maureen gathered plates, silverware and napkins. She stopped next to Daniel as she headed toward the dining room table. "You're leaving right after dinner, right?"

"Of course." He grinned, obviously liking the corner he'd backed her into. "Your boyfriend should be here any moment."

"My boyfriend has a name, you know."

"Yeah. But it's more fun this way."

She grabbed the plates a little tighter. "I thought we'd called a truce."

"Are we arguing? I wasn't arguing. I was being friendly."

Her hands shook as she set the table. Why was she letting him get to her? She shouldn't give him that kind of power, but just ignore him, or tease him back.

However, six years of antagonism couldn't be erased in a day.

The doorbell rang. Grateful for the distraction, she hurried down the hall and opened the door.

"If I had my own key," Ted said, "you wouldn't have to—"

She flung herself into his arms, stopping any discussion about house keys. She had enough on her plate already.

"Well," he said, kissing her hello. "I missed you, too."

She wondered if he thought her underwear boring. Sex was fine between them. She had no complaints. Nor had he complained about the long T-shirt she wore to bed at night.

"This is nice," Ted said, "having you home so early. I'll bet Riley's happy."

Was that a subtle dig at her for not doing the same for him?

"It does feel good," she said. "Although you know I've got a few hours of work ahead after he goes to sleep."

"You don't have to remind me. I'm aware of what's expected."

"I'm sorry, sweetheart. I know this is hard on you."

"I'm doing my best to be patient," he said.

Her conversation with Cherie the night before flashed in her mind. *Did* she defer to him? How would he react if she didn't?

And *why* did she, anyway? She liked to get along with people, but *defer*?

Daniel came down the hall then. "Welcome," he said, as if he were the host or something. He passed Ted a wineglass. "I hope you like merlot. It seems to be all we've got."

We've? Maureen reacted to the proprietary word.

"It's what we both like," Ted said woodenly. "That's why *we* have it."

It was apparent she couldn't let Daniel continue to make meals every night and do whatever other domestic chores needing doing—although it would be easy to let him, his brazen handling of her lingerie notwithstanding.

No one took care of her. Even as a child she'd been responsible for herself. Then when she lived with Cherie after Jess was born, Maureen had refused to be any kind of burden to her aunt, and did more than her fair share of the work. Having a master sergeant, a former drill instructor, for a father had instilled a strong work ethic in her.

So, maybe she was *used* to doing, not letting someone else *do*…but having Daniel take care of the meal, and even the laundry, was nice.

"Still want to criticize vegetarian meals?" Daniel asked later when they were done eating.

"Not that one," she said, although with a smile. Dinner had been delicious and filling. "I can see why it's your favorite, Riley. And your lettuce was perfect."

Riley beamed.

"I'll do the dishes," Ted announced, gathering plates and utensils. "Thank you for dinner, Daniel."

"Glad you liked it." Daniel flashed a grin at Maureen as Ted headed toward the kitchen. Ted hadn't said he liked the meal.

"Can I watch *Animal Planet?*" Riley asked.

"His favorite," Daniel mouthed to Maureen.

"Of course," she said to Riley. "Let me see what channel it's on."

"Sixty-five!"

"You've obviously made yourself at home. That's good," she said, aiming the remote control at the television, finding it already on channel sixty-five.

"Cool! I love sharks." He sat cross-legged on the couch and focused on the program.

"I can drive you to your apartment," she said to Daniel. "I see your stuff arrived. Looks like a lot to carry that far."

He glanced toward the kitchen. "I appreciate it."

"I'm taking Daniel home," she called out to Ted, who came into the doorway.

"I'll do it."

"You'll lose your parking space. My car's in the garage."

"I'll take *your* car."

Maureen didn't care for his autocratic attitude. And she especially wouldn't put up with it for six weeks. "Thanks, anyway. You want to go?" she asked Riley.

"Where?"

"I'm going to drop your grandpa off at his apartment."

"Do I have to? They're going to trap the shark in the cage."

"Do you mind if Riley stays here?" she asked Ted. "I'll only be gone about ten minutes."

"No."

No, he didn't mind or no, something else? She ignored it. "Ready?" she asked Daniel, who seemed to be enjoying the exchange.

He gave Riley a smacking kiss and hug, then grabbed his suitcases and followed her out. "I didn't notice a garage," he said as they walked down the steps.

"I rent space from my neighbor two doors down." She dug the garage door opener from her purse and aimed it. "I take public transportation a lot. Finding parking is one of the great quests in San Francisco."

Daniel fit one suitcase in the trunk and one in the back seat. "Alone at last," he said, after he slipped into the passenger seat.

She looked sharply at him. He was smiling. She really didn't know what to make of him, he was so unpredictable and, well, indecipherable. "Jess left a message on my voice mail at work saying she arrived in L.A. fine."

"Good."

She backed up the short driveway, then headed out. "Did Riley ask about her today?"

"Several times." He laid a hand on her shoulder. "He'll be okay. He's got us."

She didn't know what to do with a subdued Daniel. She only knew she didn't want him touching her, had avoided that ever since a few years back when she'd been visiting Jess and had almost fallen. Daniel had caught her, steadied her, then had taken his time letting her go.

"And Ted," she added.

"Yeah." He took away his hand. A few beats passed. "Not used to kids, is he?"

"No. But he's trying. He got tickets for the three of us to see a Giants game next Saturday."

Another pause. "Okay."

She glanced at him. "Not a good idea?"

"I didn't say that."

"Your silence did."

"So, now you can read my mind?"

"Hardly."

He grinned.

"So, again I ask, is it not a good idea?"

"For the first three innings, maybe."

She'd been afraid of that. Ted had gotten the tickets without asking, thinking it would be a nice surprise, without knowing if Riley even liked baseball. Not to mention completely ignoring her usual Saturday activity of delivering meals with Cherie. "It'll be something different to do," she said finally.

"Yes, it will."

"Everything working out with the apartment?"

"So far, so good. I'm not expecting much, so it'll probably live up to expectation."

"How will you spend your evenings?"

"Are you kidding? This is San Francisco. I don't figure I'll be home much at all."

His enthusiasm stirred up a little envy. She'd been grateful for Ted coming along when he had, at a time when she'd about given up on finding Mr. Right, but they spent a lot of time at home, not getting out in the beautiful city they lived in. She was usually too tired, for one thing, after putting in such long hours at work. But that would settle down sometime—possibly when Bernadette announced who would be the new vice president, but probably not until the two new projects they were working on hit the market. The company was expanding fast, maybe too fast without adding staff.

"Why so quiet?" Daniel asked as she double-parked in front of his apartment.

"Just thinking about how life changes so quickly."

"Adapt or atrophy. Those are our choices, I think."

She smiled. "Similar to the publish or perish in your line of work."

"Exactly. Thanks for the ride, Maureen."

"You're welcome. Thanks for dinner."

"And doing the laundry?"

She'd forgotten. Even now she felt her face warm, but she refused to let him feel any sense of triumph. "Thank you."

He laughed then opened the door. When he had both suitcases on the sidewalk he leaned into the car. "I was serious about the lacy lingerie."

"I'm not discussing my lingerie with you."

"Just trying to be helpful. Most women could benefit from a man's advice on some things."

"Well, gee. Lucky me. I got it for free."

His eyes twinkled. "Looking out for your best interests. Men are pretty basic. It's better if you women understand that."

"I'll take it under advisement." She certainly wouldn't invest in lacy underwear while there was any possibility he might do her laundry again. But maybe after he was gone…

"See you in the morning." He started to shut the door, then crouched down. "I know our relationship has been a little antagonistic—"

"A little?"

"I understand how you feel," he went on, ignoring her. "But I don't think you've given a lot of thought to how I feel. Your daughter is alive. You got a chance to raise her. Neither is true for me about Josh. Riley is all I have left of him."

"I have all the sympathy in the world for you about losing your son, Daniel. It's the way you went about enticing Jess to move to Seattle, and how you've continued—" She stopped before she started lecturing him. It wasn't the time or place. "It doesn't matter right now, you know? As you've pointed out, Riley needs for us to get along. He comes first."

He hesitated, then finally stood. "It'll work even better if we get along because *we* want to. Good night."

She saw him in her rearview mirror, watching until she

drove off. She let out a long breath. He'd always gotten under her skin, so why should it be any different this time?

And this time it was even worse—it wasn't a week but six weeks. She couldn't ignore him or keep her distance. Nor could she totally ignore what happened to her physically whenever he was near.

Maureen pulled into the garage, then went inside her house. Riley and Ted were intent on the television program, but then Riley spotted her and grinned. Ted spotted her and frowned.

Maureen moved to give them both hugs.

Three days down, thirty-nine to go.

CHAPTER 6

Rileyism #8: "What's a bane, Papa?"

"How long are you going to wait to tell Bernadette about the baby?" Maureen asked Anza over lunch a few days later. They were seated in a taqueria near work, where they often had lunch.

"A couple of months, I think. I want to be sure everything is okay."

"She's not going to be surprised. We all know you want children." Maureen studied Anza as she picked up her substantial chicken-and-cheese burrito and took a bite. "I'm astounded that you can down that with such gusto. I don't think I ate anything but crackers and, oddly enough, watermelon during the first three months of my pregnancy."

"I am starved all the time."

"Well then, I kind of doubt you'll be able to keep the pregnancy secret for much longer if you continue eating like that. Not to mention you're already stretching the buttonholes on your blouse."

"And Gabe is giddy about that." She grinned. "Or he would be if I could stand to let him touch me."

Maureen remembered, too, how painful her breasts were. At seventeen, she'd known nothing about being pregnant. Everything had surprised her. If she hadn't had her aunt guiding her, she would've stayed ignorant and in denial about everything. Because of Cherie, Maureen had financial and emotional security. "Are you going to continue to work after the baby's born?"

"Can't afford not to. But I'm hoping that Bernadette will let me work from home some of the time. I can research on my home computer as easily as at the office. And proofread, for that matter. And edit. Maybe three days a week at home? Or maybe just mornings or afternoons? I don't dare talk to her about it yet, not until things settle down."

"I'm wondering if they ever will." Maureen stabbed a tomato among the pile of shredded lettuce of her tostada. "I'm very worried about Bernadette."

"Why?"

"She hasn't let herself grieve for Carlos. She plunged right back into work, without any time off. She's always been fun and easygoing, but now she's so stressed. Everyone has a breaking point."

"Speaking of which," Anza said. "How's it going with Daniel?"

Maureen stopped short of rolling her eyes. "I don't know what to make of him. He seems to like to embarrass me." She'd never been teased the way he teased—although that could be more because of her own personality. More than one man had accused her of being too serious, which hadn't really offended her. Life was serious. There were consequences for actions, therefore actions needed to be thought out. She'd also had a child to raise, an obligation she took seriously, especially without a husband to help parent. She let loose once a month with the Rowdies, so she knew she was capable of it, but it didn't come naturally.

"How does he embarrass you?"

She told Anza about the laundry incident.

"He actually called you *Double-D?*"

"He whispered it so that Riley couldn't hear, but yes."

"Was he looking you in the eye?"

Maureen hesitated. "I think so. I was kind of seeing red at the moment."

Anza grinned.

"Hey! Whose side are you on?" Maureen asked.

"Yours, of course. But I've always loved your Daniel stories."

"He's never grown up."

"Part of his charm, I would guess. And he's fifty, right? Hmm. You know who would be perfect for him?"

"Who?" Maureen asked, suspicious, knowing most of Anza's friends, many of whom had been part of the Rowdies at one time or another.

"Sunny. She's a runner and a vegetarian, too, remember? She's only thirty-five but I don't see that as a problem for either of them."

"Sunny? She's a man eater!"

"She just has a short attention span. Most men don't mind, and since Daniel is only here for a few more weeks and he's free in the evenings, why not hook them up?"

"My ears are burning."

Maureen jumped at the sound of Daniel's voice, laced with humor. She'd been so focused on the lunacy of Anza's idea to hook up Daniel with Sunny, of all people, that she hadn't seen Daniel and Riley come into the taqueria.

"Hi, Grandma. We're on a field trip."

Maureen put an arm around him and brought him close. "Another one? What's today's adventure?"

"We came to see where you work."

"We did call," Daniel said. "Someone in your office told me we could find you here." He zeroed in on Anza. "Hi, I'm Daniel, the bane of Maureen's existence."

They shook hands.

"What's a bane, Papa?"

"Someone who likes to joke around a lot," Maureen answered before looking at Anza. "This is Riley. Riley, this is my very best friend, Esperanza Ochoa."

"That's a long name."

"It sure is. You can call me Anza."

"Okay." Riley gave Maureen a funny look. "I thought Ted was your very best friend, Grandma."

"No, he's my boyfriend." The unasked question hung in the air like an invisible accusation: Shouldn't Ted, as her boyfriend, also be her best friend?

Apparently Daniel and Anza were having the same thought, as they both eyed her curiously.

"Mommy said my daddy was her very best friend. Did you know my daddy?"

Maureen's heart gave a little thump at the memories that flashed before her. She didn't dare look at Daniel. "I sure did. If you want, we can talk about him tonight, okay? Are you hungry?"

His smile was utterly beguiling. "I like chips."

She looked at Daniel. "Have you eaten?"

"Nope." He pulled out a chair and sat, as did Riley, his feet dangling and swinging as he grabbed a tortilla chip from the basket and bit into it, splintering the crunchy chip into fragments that dropped onto his clothing and the floor. Daniel signaled the waitress for a menu. They discussed ingredients and preparation, then he settled on a cheese enchilada with a bowl of pinto beans with onions and peppers on the side. Riley ordered a chicken taco.

"So, Riley eats meat?" Anza asked.

"Not a lot of it, but yes. You're a big fish-eater, aren't you, bud?"

He crunched on another chip and nodded his head several times. "I like slimehead the best."

Maureen and Anza looked to Daniel.

"A kid-friendly term for orange roughy," he supplied with a grin. "So...who are you hooking me up with?"

"My friend Sunny," Anza said before Maureen could answer—or refuse to. "You have a lot in common."

"Yeah?" He gave Maureen a look she couldn't decipher. "Like what?"

"She's a goer and doer like you. Very athletic. Eats healthy, although she lectures about it a lot, which can be really annoying. Do you lecture?"

"Only in the classroom. I'm sure my students sometimes find me annoying. So, is she attractive?"

"If you like the type," Maureen said.

"What type would that be?"

"I hafta go to the bathroom," Riley said, hopping down from his chair and heading toward the back of the restaurant.

Daniel rushed to catch up.

"Why are you doing that?" Maureen asked Anza.

"Doing what?"

"Setting him up with Sunny when it's obvious I don't want you to?"

"Why don't you?"

"He's more than capable of finding a woman for himself."

Anza sat back. "Oh…my…God. You're jealous."

"Don't be ridiculous."

"Don't lie."

Maureen watched the doorway where Daniel and Riley disappeared, not wanting to get caught by surprise again. "I've got Ted, for heaven's sake."

Anza gave her a long, steady look. "Okay, maybe not Sunny. How about I set him up with Teresa instead?"

"Teresa? That's ridiculous!" Maureen pictured the man-crazy woman with the hourglass figure. Men literally tripped when they saw her walking down the street. "She's no more suited than—" Maureen clamped her mouth shut as Anza smiled with Cheshire-cat satisfaction. "He's a big boy, Anza. Let him do his own shopping. Please."

"I will, but—" she leaned forward "—you'd better take a good look at why you're so against it."

Why *was* she? Actually, it could work in her favor if Daniel met someone here, fell in love and moved to San Francisco, because Jess and Riley would probably move, too.

That idea stuck in her head through the rest of lunch, and even later as they all walked to Primero. Anza disappeared into her office. Maureen introduced Riley and Daniel to much of the staff as they headed toward her own office. Bernadette was in a meeting.

Maureen handed Daniel a foldout brochure. "Here's what we're focused on now, and why we're all working such long hours."

He scanned it. "ShortTakes? I've never heard of them."

"They're going to hit the market in August."

"Ah. Just in time for school to start. So, Primero has gotten into the cheat-sheet business after all these years of being a legitimate reference-book publisher. What would your founder think?"

"They're *study guides*, designed to be used in conjunction with reading the work," she said defensively of the product that wasn't as detailed as Cliff's Notes nor as condensed as some of the other publications. She sat Riley at her desk with some paper and colored pens. "And Carlos was the one who came up with the idea. We're just following through." She pushed a book at Daniel then. "This is the other project he started that we're about ready to go to market with."

"*The Goof-Proof Guide to Investments*. I take it you're going to publish a whole slew of Goof-Proof Guides?"

"We're introducing twenty titles in September, and planning on putting out four new ones a month after that."

"Isn't the market saturated enough?" He thumbed through the volume, stopping and reading now and then.

"Ours are much more accessible."

"Meaning, you dumbed them down?"

"Not at all. They're just updated versions of the reference books we've done all these years, with a lot more bulleted lists, for the way people absorb information these days."

"Strike while the iron is hot."

"It's just good business. I realize as an English professor you probably hate the idea of the ShortTakes…."

"You're right." He handed back the book and brochure. "I imagine you'll be very successful."

"But?"

"But nothing. Free enterprise is a cornerstone of our country."

"But?"

"I'm old school." He shrugged. "I think you don't appreciate things unless you do the work."

Maureen took a mental step back. His free-spirit personality had always made him seem like someone who didn't mind cutting corners here and there.

"Hey, bud," Daniel said. "We should let your grandma get back to work."

"But I'm not done."

"You can take it with you," Maureen said, kissing the top of his head. She glanced at his drawing—stick figures scattered around the page, mostly in pairs. "Who are all these people?"

He pointed. "Me and my best friend, Cody. Mommy and Daddy. You and Anzi."

"Anza."

"Oh, yeah." He tapped his pen on a lone male. "This is Papa. He needs Willy next to him."

"Something you haven't told me?" Maureen asked Daniel.

He laughed. "My dog. Named for Shakespeare. A friend is fostering him until I go home."

She noticed Ted wasn't anywhere in the picture. His difficulty relating to children, Riley included, probably didn't make him memorable to a six-year-old child.

"I don't remember your having a dog."

"He's new. Golden retriever. Into chewing slippers for entertainment."

Slippers? She couldn't picture it. Even now Daniel wore ratty jeans and his Cascade University sweatshirt that had seen better days. He tended to wear running shoes or go barefoot. Slippers? Nope.

"He likes to lick your face," Riley added with a giggle. "Sloppy kisses. Mommy is gonna let me get a dog when she comes home. It's 'spensive to have a dog. When she wins a bazillion dollars, we're gonna go get us a dog, first thing."

Maureen had never owned a dog. Or a cat. Not even as a child. Even though Jess had begged for a dog, Maureen hadn't gotten her one, thinking the city wasn't a great place to have one—even though they had a nice backyard.

How much had she denied Jess because she'd needed to maintain such tight control over the course of their lives? She'd been so afraid of making any more mistakes, with Jess paying for them.

Lessons learned, she'd thought then, not mistakes. But now, looking back? Had Jess rebelled so much because Maureen had been too rigid, like she'd rebelled against her father?

She laid her hands on Riley's shoulders. "A dog would be good."

"I'll be 'sponsible, Grandma."

"I'm sure you will."

"Let's go, bud."

Riley planted a smacking kiss on Maureen's cheek, then hugged her, bringing tears to her eyes. It was the most spontaneous affection he'd shown since he'd arrived.

"I love you," she said, squeezing him.

"Love you, too." He walked over to Daniel. "You kiss her goodbye, too."

Daniel's eyes gleamed as he leaned over and kissed Maureen's cheek. A scud missile might as well have been launched at her. Heat exploded from within in a huge, fiery blast that caught her by surprise. She'd always been aware of…stirrings when he was around, but not like this. Nothing like this. And she'd always chalked it up to anger…. Or had held on to the anger rather than acknowledge any other emotion.

Daniel headed toward the door then glanced back, Riley's hand in his. "There's some stew left over from last night. I'll be taking off as soon as you get home."

"Thanks." She could hear them saying goodbye to her coworkers as they made their way through the office. She plopped into her chair. This was bad. Really bad. The only other time she'd had a physical reaction that strong over such little contact was with Kirk, Jess's father.

And look where that got me.

Plus Daniel had looked totally unaffected, just slightly entertained by Riley's demand.

Her direct line rang. The caller ID spelled out Ted's name.

Reliable, steady, structured Ted, a man with traits so similar to hers they'd seemed destined from their first meeting. Forget the old opposites-attract theory. It'd been proven over and over that people who had a lot in common stuck together.

"Hi, sweetheart," she said, settling back in her chair.

"How's your day going?"

Yeah. This was good. Easy and comfortable. No scud missiles in sight.

It was the best route to a happy life.

CHAPTER 7

Rileyism #12: "He's not a bane at all, Grandma."

"I wanna go home." Riley leaned heavily against Maureen. He'd gotten whinier by the inning, which was now the sixth.

"Barry Bonds will be at bat next," Ted said tightly. "Maybe he'll hit a home run."

"Again? He already got one."

"No one would mind if he hit one every time he got up to bat." Ted smiled slightly at Maureen.

Riley shrugged. "Can I have some more peanuts, Grandma?"

Maureen knew Riley wasn't really hungry but bored. Cracking peanuts out of their shells gave him something to do, especially since he was allowed to drop the shells on the ground. "But that's littering," he'd said at first. Once he saw everyone else doing it, he joined in, laughing about it.

"Why don't you and I head over to the kids' area and play for a while?" she said, looking over his head at Ted.

"O-kay!"

"We'll be back by the top of the ninth, Ted."

"That's okay. I'll find you after the game's over. How about at the superslide?"

"Works for me." She leaned over Riley's head and gave Ted a kiss. "Thanks."

"Do you think he'll even remember coming here?"

"Hard to tell with kids. *I* appreciate your efforts."

He focused on the action. She took Riley's hand and maneuvered down the row to the aisle, wondering what Riley would tell Daniel about their day at the game. Then again, by Monday, a whole two days off, Riley might have forgotten. Daniel had been right. Three innings was Riley's limit for paying attention to a game he didn't know much about. The hat and mitt Ted had bought him were slight diversions. He'd wanted a ball, too, but Ted had vetoed that for fear Riley would lose it during the game— or bonk someone on the head with it. Ted promised to buy him one after the game, which Maureen thought was a great compromise.

Since she wasn't really a baseball fan herself, she was glad to go off with Riley to the Little Giants Park. On the way there her cell phone rang. Anza's name flashed.

"What's up?"

"You have to get down here right away, Maureen."

She kept her eyes on Riley, who skipped ahead of her. "Where?"

"The office. Everyone's been called in."

"On a Saturday? Why? What's going on?" They'd managed to avoid working on Saturdays and Sundays by putting in the late hours during the week.

"Some major computer meltdown."

"What could I do to help that? Or you, for that matter?"

"Bernadette issued the order. I'm just the messenger. Don't shoot."

"I'm at the Giants' game with Riley and Ted."

"How much do you want the promotion?"

She wanted it so much she could already picture the nameplate on her office door: Maureen Hart, Vice President, Operations. "I'll see what I can do. I'll call you back in a few minutes." She snapped her phone shut and called out to Riley. "C'mere. We need to go talk to Ted for a minute."

"But, Grandma—"

"I know. I'm sorry." She held out her hand. He ignored it and stomped ahead of her. They slid into their seats next to a surprised Ted. She explained the situation.

"I don't understand what you want me to do, Maureen."

"Help me decide. I'm tempted to tell them I can't come in, period. The other alternative would be for all three of us to leave, or I could catch a cab on my own, then you could bring Riley home after the game." She knew he didn't appreciate the options, but she wondered which one was the least objectionable. No matter which choice they made, he would have to watch Riley.

"We might as well go together."

"I'm so sorry, Ted. I'll make it up to you."

He waited until they'd walked up the stairs to the concourse before he put his arm around her and leaned close. "Maybe you could get a babysitter and come to my place? It's been a while. I've missed you."

"You mean I don't get to go on the big slide?" Riley interrupted.

"I'm sorry, sweetie. Not this time. Grandma has to go to the office."

He started to cry. He hadn't had a nap, because the game had started about the time he usually rested. He'd eaten peanuts, a hot dog, a pretzel and soda, not exactly his usual balanced diet. And he was disappointed. The car ride home looked to be tense.

She knelt down and hugged him, aware that she hadn't answered Ted about their getting together. He was right. They hadn't made love since Riley's arrival. She hadn't even missed it, a staggering thought in itself. She'd been so filled with spending every second with Riley that she'd ignored Ted. Plus she'd had to work late at night after Riley went to bed. She also didn't want Ted spending the night with Riley there, not wanting to set a bad example. But she couldn't ignore Ted completely, either. That wasn't fair.

Riley continued to sob into her shoulder.

"Do you still want a baseball?" Ted asked him.

He lifted his head a little. "Y-y-yes."

"We'll be leaving the park through the Dugout store. You need to stop crying so you can see the balls to choose one."

Maureen appreciated his patience as well as the ploy. So,

maybe it was bribery. A disappointed six-year-old was not a pretty sight to behold.

When they pulled up in front of her office later, she glanced at a sleeping Riley in the back seat. "I don't know how to thank you, Ted."

"Yes, you do." He ran his hand down her hair. His thumb caressed her cheek. "I imagine Daniel would be happy to stay overnight at your house so that we could have some time together."

Maureen was sure of it. "I'll be too tired tonight, even if Daniel was available on such short notice."

"Tomorrow, then."

"We'll talk about it. I know this has been hard on you. I'm really sorry about that." But not about having Riley there. No, not sorry about that at all. They were getting closer every day.

It struck her then that she was repeating the pattern from when Jess was little. Maureen had dated, but she'd never really gotten close to any man in particular, because Jess had always come first. Maureen had protected her daughter from the men who came in and out of her life, many of whom would've stayed longer except that she'd kept them at arm's length and they gave up.

It was futile to regret what was past, but if she had it to do over again? She'd do it a little differently, she realized. Let herself have more fun, which would've spilled over to Jess.

"I'll stay away tomorrow and let you and Riley have the

day together," Ted said. "But I want to see you tomorrow night. If Daniel can't watch Riley, you can find someone else. Your aunt would probably be delighted." He added, "Okay?" a little too late.

"I'll try. Thanks again for everything. I'll give you a call when I know what's going on here, and how long it's going to take. Talk to you later."

"I need a key," he said before she shut the door. It wasn't hard to interpret his tone—if she'd given him a key to her house before, he wouldn't have to ask. They hadn't talked about the key situation since he'd given her his. She slid her key ring into his hand without comment.

Tension vibrated in the air when Maureen stepped inside the building. Everyone glanced at her as she passed by on her way to Bernadette's office, but no one spoke.

"I'm here," she said to Bernadette, who sat at her desk surrounded by paperwork and CDs.

"Nice of you to join us."

The sarcasm caught Maureen off guard. Bernadette was always polite and appreciative. The problems must be huge for her to speak to Maureen like that.

"I'm sorry. I was at the Giants' game with my grandson. I left as soon as—"

Bernadette cut her off with a gesture. "I need you to do what everyone else is doing—make sure all your work has been backed up and saved. D.J. will run a check on your computer, then you'll need to reinstall everything. We've had a crash like you wouldn't believe, network wide."

"I back up every day before I leave."

Bernadette gave her a look that didn't need interpretation. Maureen went to Anza's office. Her expression was grim.

"I don't know that woman," Anza whispered, hitching a thumb toward Bernadette's office.

"She's scared, and she feels alone. This was Carlos's baby. He always handled the crises."

"Then she needs to hire someone to help her. You missed her storming-through-the-office rant."

"Give her a break, Anza. Everything's on her shoulders."

"She needs to learn to delegate more."

"I agree." Maureen headed to her office, where for hours she installed and checked files against written records. Her job as liaison between Primero and the freelance writers was a critical one, and her records of every phone conversation and written communication were extensive and detailed. After she was done with her own work, she helped the Accounting department.

By the time Maureen dragged herself home it was almost ten o'clock. Ted was watching television, which he turned off right away. He had put away all evidence that a six-year-old boy lived there. She'd relaxed her need for neatness since Riley's arrival, not minding the clutter that came with him. Ted minded. Although she had to admit sometimes the disorganization got to her, too.

Had Jess resented her for that, too? Probably. Jess ran a much more relaxed household.

Maureen glanced at Riley's bedroom door.

"He went down a couple hours ago," Ted said. "Not willingly or happily."

She hugged him, but her thoughts weren't on him. "He fights it every night."

"He said his mother lets him stay up as long as he wants."

Maureen laughed. "Yeah, he's tried that on me, too."

"Do you think it's true?"

"No. He was just testing you to see what he could get away with."

"Guess I failed."

"Or passed, depending on how you look at it." She sank into the chair Ted had vacated and leaned her head back, closing her eyes. "I am wiped out. How'd you spend the evening?"

"We walked down to the video store and picked up a couple of DVDs. He chose them. I just checked to make sure they were rated G. They really do make inane movies for kids, don't they?"

She smiled. "I haven't watched any lately. We've been too busy playing cars and games at night, I guess."

"I don't know how to do that."

She opened her eyes at the flatness in his voice. "I wasn't criticizing, Ted. I'm sure he enjoyed watching the movies."

He sat on the edge of the sofa and leaned toward her. "I know in your eyes he's a little prince."

"What does that mean?"

"Just stating a fact. But to me, he was rude. Wouldn't

answer my questions, wouldn't help pick up his toys before he went to bed. Sassed me."

"He wants to know his limits with you."

"He found them."

She frowned. "What happened?"

"I yelled at him. I know, I know. He's just a little boy. I apologized to him. I've never been around kids, Maureen. I didn't know they test. I just knew he was driving me crazy. Things were fine between us by the time he went to bed."

Since Ted had never raised his voice to Maureen, she couldn't picture the scenario. But he was six-three and towered over Riley. Had he been afraid?

Her exhaustion deepened. She felt as if she were defending and excusing everyone *to* everyone—Bernadette, Riley, even Ted and Daniel. Herself, for that matter. It wore her out. Where was the fun she used to have? Going to work used to be fun. Her life had been— Well, maybe it hadn't been tons of fun, but more so than now.

How could she fix it?

She knew Ted was waiting for her to say something to make it all better for him, to excuse him for having yelled at Riley. He seemed to be seeking her forgiveness. "I'm sure Riley will have forgotten all about it in the morning, Ted. It was good you apologized."

"My point, Maureen, is that the boy needs to be taught to respect his elders, and to do what they say."

"He's only six."

"Old enough for manners."

Her instinct was to defend Riley, her recent M.O. She stood instead. "I need to go to bed."

They stared at each other for several long seconds, then he stood, as well. She walked him to the door.

"You're mad at me," he said, holding her hand.

Was that it? She didn't think it was that simple. "I'm just tired."

"I only want to know where I fit in, Maureen. As long as Riley's here, what's my place in your life?"

"It's whatever you want it to be. Be involved or keep your distance. It's entirely up to you."

He let go of her hand. "I wish he'd never come," he said, then left without kissing her goodbye.

Anger burned a slow path through her. So Ted resented Riley because his visit had changed his life in ways he didn't like. Of all the selfish—

Maureen shoved her hair back from her face, trying to see the situation from Ted's perspective. He didn't understand about Jess and Riley, didn't know how devastated Maureen had been when Jess chose to take her newborn son to Seattle to live with Daniel, a man she hardly knew, except that he was Josh's father—absentee father. Daniel had swooped into their lives and taken charge. Maureen hadn't known what hit her until there was only silence in her house instead of her daughter and grandson filling up space, bringing an abundance of life.

Daniel had stolen that from her. She'd harbored such resentment toward him for so long. Even now he was interfering. He should've stayed away and let her have Riley to herself. Even Jess had wanted that.

But he'd stayed. And she'd let him. Maybe her anger was as much about resenting Daniel as it was about Ted resenting Riley. Maybe she needed to have it out with Daniel so that she could put it behind her. Resentment had eaten away at her, not a healthy situation.

It was time to let it go.

But still, her irritation with Ted lingered. He'd gotten tickets to the Giants' game without asking her first, not taking into consideration her usual Saturday plans, as if they didn't matter. He'd yelled at Riley.

That situation needed to be dealt with, too, and soon.

After checking on Riley, she went to bed. She was almost asleep when she heard her door open. A moment later she felt him get into bed and snuggle close.

"Grandma?" he whispered.

"What, sweetie?"

"That man? You know—your boyfriend?"

"Ted?"

"Yeah."

"What about him?"

"He's not a bane, you know, Grandma. He's not fun at all."

"I'm sorry."

He sighed. "I miss Mommy."

"Me, too."

"I miss Daddy, too. I wish I could see him."

Maureen's eyes stung at the longing in his voice. What could she say?

Before she could come up with something, she felt him relax against her then fall asleep.

She wished she could say the same for herself.

CHAPTER 8

Rileyism #13: "Are you gonna sleep with Grandma?"

Maureen spent Sunday enjoying her grandson. She turned off her cell phone and took Riley to Pier 39 to watch the sea lions sun themselves on the floating docks, then took him on a boat tour around the San Francisco Bay. There was no pressure from anyone, no competition for attention, just a slow, easy day of companionship. If there was a cloud above number nine, she was on it.

They got home in time for Riley to take a bath before bed. He conked out instantly.

All day she'd avoided calling Ted. He'd expected her to arrange for Daniel or Cherie to spend the night with Riley, but Maureen decided she didn't want to go to Ted's house and…placate him. It was cowardly to avoid him. With Riley asleep, she finally pushed the message button on her answering machine.

"Why aren't you answering your cell phone?" Ted asked, his message similar to the three he'd left on her voice mail.

"We're not fighting, are we? Are you coming over tonight? Call me."

A couple of hang-ups followed. Ted, she supposed.

Maureen lay down on the couch and closed her eyes. *Were* they fighting? It was the first time they'd disagreed about anything of importance. Cherie had commented on how Maureen deferred to Ted. It was true. She liked peaceful relationships, not conflict. She'd had conflict her entire childhood and had vowed to keep it out of her life. It helped that she rarely saw her father, although he lived less than forty minutes away. They got together at Christmas at Cherie's house, his birthday and sometimes on Father's Day, although not this year. They had little to say to each other.

Maureen's rift with her daughter wasn't anywhere near as bad—

Someone knocked on the front door. She glanced at her watch. Almost nine o'clock.

"Hey," Daniel said, standing with his hands in his pockets and wearing a baseball cap turned backward. She wanted to tell him to grow up, but he did look kind of cute wearing the cap like that.

"Is this a bad time? I didn't see Ted's car. I tried to call, but you didn't pick up on either phone."

"I didn't want to be disturbed."

He grinned, which made her smile back reluctantly and feel foolish besides.

"Did you have a good day?" he asked.

"We did."

"Can I come in?"

She stepped back, holding the door open.

"I think it's time we clear the air," he said.

Oh, she hated that he'd beaten her to the punch. She'd fully intended to do just that, and now he would never believe that it'd been her plan, too.

"We've never talked about my son," he said, taking a seat on the sofa.

"Riley is talking a lot about him. Is that something new?"

"Yeah. I'm not sure what triggered it. Jess and I have always talked to him about Josh, but now Riley's asking questions and wanting to see pictures. Josh's mother had videotapes, and Riley watches them a lot. So do I, frankly. I barely knew my son."

Maureen sat on the opposite end of the sofa, tucking her legs under her and dragging a pillow into her lap. "He and Jess dated for over a year before…he died. He didn't talk much about you. I'm so sorry, Daniel," she said quickly when he winced. "I didn't say that to hurt you. I meant I didn't know why you weren't part of his life. He didn't talk about it."

"His mother kept us apart. That's the short version."

"I wouldn't mind hearing the long version."

He leaned forward, resting his elbows on his thighs. "The long version is that Kelly and I met while we were in the master's program at Notre Dame, English for me, American history for her. We got married and started teaching at the same community college. Two years later we found out she was pregnant on the same day that I was accepted into the Ph.D. program at Notre Dame. We knew it was going to be a struggle, but we decided it was worth it. I wanted to teach at university level. A year into the program, Kelly decided it was time to have another baby. I disagreed. I wanted to finish the program, which would take another three years or so."

"Makes sense."

"Thank you." He dragged his hands down his face and blew out a breath. "She didn't agree. She made things increasingly difficult at home, then decided it was her or the Ph.D. By then I was only two years away from completion. I couldn't believe she was delivering that kind of ultimatum. It wasn't her or the degree, it was her *and Josh* or the degree. Josh was two. He was starting to talk. He'd become his own person. God, he was cute. Towheaded and brilliant blue eyes. An infectious, rollicking laugh. He'd fly into my arms to greet me." He hesitated. "She stole him away from me."

"What do you mean?"

"I came home one day and they were gone. She'd gotten another teaching position in another state without telling me she'd applied. She'd also filed for divorce."

Maureen noted a lack of emotion in his voice and wondered at it. Because it had been so long ago, or maybe because he needed to hide his pain?

"Why would she do that without telling you?" she asked.

"I finally came to realize—years later, mind you—that it

had little to do with me. Everything was fine with Kelly as long as she was getting her way. My getting the Ph.D. meant I would have more status, at least in academic circles. She couldn't deal with that."

"Yet she agreed that you should go back to school."

He looked away. "I'm not sure that's true. It could very well be that I told her what my plans were, without consulting her much. I saw things with blinders on then."

"Only then?"

He ignored her gentle jibe. "I saw Josh as much as I could, then after I finished the program I got a position at a university near them. By the next school year, she was gone again. New job, new town. A year later I followed. A year later she was off to Seattle. I followed again.

"A year later she moved to San Francisco. By then I'd figured out it would be a lifetime of cat-and-mouse. I liked where I was teaching, but more important, I wanted Josh to be able to stay put so that he could at least go to middle school and high school in the same city, and have the same friends. I thought I was doing the right thing for my son."

"That makes sense."

He focused on her then. "I always wondered… Why didn't you follow Jess and Riley to Seattle?"

Why hadn't she? She'd never spelled it out for herself. "In the beginning I was too hurt by her leaving. But I think the real reason was because I always figured it was temporary, that she would come back."

"Then she didn't."

"Time kept passing. I recognized it by how much Riley grew in between visits. Still, I thought they would come home."

"And now? What do you think?"

"That they've made a life in Seattle. This isn't home anymore." It was hard for Maureen to admit it, that her daughter didn't need her.

"In a way, that's how I felt, too," he said. "Especially when Kelly remarried, and Josh started calling the guy Dad. I thought that was the worst that could happen, but the worst came a little later when my son told me he didn't want to see me anymore, that I complicated his life. He had a full-time dad now. I was expendable.

"In hindsight I realize I was wrong not to keep following them, thinking I was making his life easier, more consistent. I should've gone wherever he moved. But I backed off. I figured in a few years he would graduate and I would make a push then. I thought if I were persistent enough...

"Then he and Kelly were killed in the car accident, and I never got that chance to reunite with him. Of course, no one bothered to tell me about Jess and her pregnancy. I found out only after Riley was born. He was all I had left of my son. I had so much to make up for. So much I'd missed."

"Kelly was a difficult woman," Maureen said, remembering her. "She wouldn't give her permission for Josh to marry. He did live long enough to see his son, but just barely. Long enough to claim Riley as his. Then you claimed him. And Jess."

Daniel stood and walked to the window. His jaw flexed.

"Jess was looking for a father—for herself and for her baby. And Riley was all I had left of Josh. What father would turn that down? Did I go overboard? Maybe. But I'm not sorry. I'll never be sorry."

Maureen didn't know what to say. He hid a lot of heartbreak with his devil-may-care attitude. Why hadn't Jess told her?

Why hadn't she asked him herself?

"To be honest," he continued, "I haven't thought much of you, either, for denying Jess her father, since I've been there, done that, on the flip side of the situation."

The statement caught her off guard. She never talked about Jess's father. Even Jess didn't ask about him anymore. "You don't know anything about that, Daniel. Nothing."

In the heavy silence the doorbell rang. She looked at her watch. "Who could that be this late?"

She hadn't turned on the porch light so she couldn't see from the living room window to who was at the door. She walked down the hallway, could hear Daniel following, although not dogging her footsteps.

She was stunned to see Ted when she opened the door.

"So, you're alive," he said coolly, then spotted Daniel.

"I can—" *Explain*, she started to stay but Ted smiled and extended his hand to Daniel.

"Thanks for helping out," Ted said. "Maureen and I appreciate it."

"Um, sure," Daniel said.

"I must've missed your call while I was on my way here,"

Ted said to her. "Are you ready to go? Have you got your clothes for work tomorrow?"

Maureen was stuck between the rock of feeling guilty about not having called him and the hard place of his blatant expectation that she would go with him, just like that. It was her fault, of course, for not letting him know she wasn't going to spend the night, that she hadn't asked anyone to stay with Riley.

Then there was Daniel, covering for her without knowing what was going on. She couldn't exactly turn to him and ask him to stay, because Ted would pick up on that. Nor did she want to go to Ted's.

What *did* she want?

A full night's sleep in my own bed.

Both men waited for her to speak. She didn't want Daniel to witness a scene between her and Ted, but if she asked Daniel to leave, a scene would ensue.

"Grandma?" Riley poked his head around the doorway. His voice was quiet and strained. "I had a bad dream."

"Oh, sweetie. I'm sorry." She went down on her knees. He flung himself against her and pressed his face along her neck, his skin clammy.

"I was scared."

"You're okay. Dreams aren't real, remember? They're just movies in our heads."

"It was real."

"What was it about?"

He didn't answer right away. "I don't 'member. Hi, Papa."

"Hey, bud. You okay?"

He nodded. Maureen stood, but Riley clutched her hand still.

"Your grandpa's going to spend the night with you," Ted said.

"You are, Papa?"

"Um, yeah." He sent a quick look toward Maureen, one that said, "You're gonna owe me, big-time."

"Are you gonna sleep with Grandma?"

Maureen raised her brows at Daniel.

He looked flustered. "Um…"

"Your grandma is going to stay at my house tonight," Ted said smoothly.

"No," Riley said adamantly.

Maureen tried to soothe him. "Riley—"

He grabbed her blouse with both hands. "You hafta stay here with me and Papa."

Maureen recalled Ted's words about Riley being a prince in her eyes. She'd almost said, "And your point is?"

"I'll take Riley to his room," she said, ushering him out.

"I wanna sleep with you. I'm scared."

"I'll be right back, I promise. I'll stay with you until you go to sleep." She found Stripe and put the tiger in his arms, then drew a settling breath and returned to the entryway.

"Daniel, I appreciate your offer to stay, but I think Riley needs me tonight."

"Sure thing. I'll see you in the morning." He made a quick getaway, not even saying goodbye.

Which left Ted.

"Why am I not surprised?" He didn't sound angry, just resigned.

"I'm so sorry."

"Well, you tried. That counts."

"I need to get back to Riley. I promised I'd stay with him until he fell asleep."

Ted kissed her goodbye, putting a lot of effort into it. "Just a little sample of what you missed tonight."

She was worn-out from being torn in so many directions. Plus Daniel's explanation of his life without his son weighed on her. She just wanted to be alone.

Maureen locked the door behind him and hurried back into Riley's room. He was already asleep.

Saved by a six-year-old. She stroked his hair lightly. He moved a little, but didn't awaken.

Now she had to figure out how to explain it all to Daniel.

CHAPTER 9

Rileyism #14: "The answer is always no."

Maureen set her briefcase by the front door the next morning so that she could make a quick getaway when Daniel arrived. Time enough for explanation when she got home from work. Time enough to figure out what to say, anyway. She didn't want to be teased, either, something he would likely do.

"Where's Papa?" Riley asked from behind her, having gotten quietly out of bed.

"He's not here yet."

"Didn't he spend the night?"

"No." She took his hand and led him toward the kitchen. "Good morning. Would you like some juice?"

"Can I have some soda?"

She smiled. "What do you think the answer to that is?"

"No." He sighed. "The answer is *always* no."

"Oh, yeah. You're such a deprived child. You never get anything you want." She tugged on his hand until he smiled. He sat in a kitchen chair and she opened the refrigerator to hunt for the carton of orange juice.

"I think Papa should just live with us."

"I know. But that's not going to happen."

"See? The answer is *always* no."

"*Sometimes* the answer is no." She shut the refrigerator door, then spotted Daniel leaning against the doorjamb. "Good morning," she said evenly, wondering what he'd heard.

"Papa!" Riley flew out of his chair and into Daniel's arms. "I asked Grandma if you could live with us."

"We've talked about that before, bud. You know why I can't do that." He met Maureen's gaze directly, unsmiling.

For all that she wanted Riley to herself, the idea of Daniel also living there sounded way too appealing…and scary. He would shift the delicate balance of her life in ways she didn't think she could ever get back to normal.

"I need to go," she said. "I'll see you after work."

"Coward," she called herself as she hurried out of the house and up the street.

A few minutes later, aboard the crowded bus, Maureen stood in the aisle, holding tight to the bar as the vehicle bumped along in traffic. She nodded at a few people she recognized from their daily commute but was glad she didn't have to engage in conversation. She'd gotten off the hook last night with Ted only because he'd put his own spin on events, both when he'd seen Daniel with her and when Riley didn't want her to leave after his bad dream. She hadn't exactly lied, but she'd certainly omitted enlightening information and hadn't corrected his erroneous assumptions. She'd made sacrifices all her life, and the sacrifice of spending less time with Ted for the next few weeks was worth the benefits. She wished time would stand still, but it kept ticking away. Soon Jess would be back and Maureen's life would return to normal.

She wasn't sure she wanted normal back.

Maureen pushed open the door of her building. A new tension had settled at Primero Publishing since the computer meltdown on Saturday. Maureen could feel it, almost see it. People looked up in acknowledgment as she walked by, but few said good morning with their usual good cheer.

Maureen didn't like change or dissension, both of which hung in the air like a mythical fire-breathing creature, a little threatening to a person not known for her flexibility.

She put her purse in her office then went to say good morning to Bernadette. Hesitant, Maureen moved slowly and quietly, which is why she caught Bernadette with her face buried in her hands, her shoulders heaving, quiet sobs reaching the open doorway.

Knowing Bernadette would be upset at having been caught crying, Maureen took a quick step out of sight. She started to tiptoe away.

"I thought I heard someone," Bernadette said behind her.

"Just stopped by to say good morning."

"Please come in," Bernadette said with a sigh. "I'm sorry you witnessed my moment of weakness."

"Actually, I was glad about that. I've been afraid you weren't mourning."

"I mourn plenty, believe me. But in private, usually."

She sat in her chair, putting the desk between them, establishing distance physically and probably emotionally. "I apologize for sniping at you on Saturday."

"It's no problem." She didn't know whether to sit or stay standing. In the past she would've sat without being asked.

"How are things going with your grandson?"

"Better than I'd hoped, thanks. We're getting closer by the day. I really appreciate—"

Bernadette cut her off with a weary gesture. "I know you're probably getting tired of waiting for a decision on the promotion."

"I'm more curious about why you haven't decided."

"It's a tough decision. You, Doug and Ginny are equally qualified."

Maureen didn't think so. Doug was office manager and had good knowledge of how the staff worked, but not the big corporate picture. Ginny had knowledge of the financial end, a qualification critical to the job of vice president of operations, but her people skills were lacking. Maureen had been the receptionist, file clerk, accounting clerk, assistant to the vice president of sales and marketing, and for the past few years, project/author liaison. She had a broader knowledge than the other two candidates.

She was also less educated.

"How are the vacation plans going?" Bernadette asked.

"Everything is reconfirmed." Why wasn't she being invited to sit down? "After ShortTakes and the Goof-Proof Guides are released, are you going to take a break?"

"The implication being that I need to?"

"I—"

"It's okay. You've been a friend for a long time. I know you're concerned. I'm okay, Maureen. Really. Tell the others."

There was dismissal in her voice, so Maureen left her office and headed for her own. It was five minutes before eight and everyone was at their desks, whether out of devotion or fear, Maureen wasn't sure. It used to be devotion.

Her phone rang the second she sat down. "Good morning, Auntie."

A couple of beats passed, then, "It freaks me out that you know I'm on the phone before you even answer it."

Maureen leaned back and smiled. "Freaks you out?"

"Hey, my generation was using that term before yours."

"It just sounds strange out of the mouth of a seventy-year-old woman. Which is why you do it, of course."

"Busted."

Maureen laughed. "What's up?"

"I was wondering if you could meet me for lunch today?"

"Sure. Where?"

"How about Dolores Park? I'll bring the food."

"That's a deal and a half. I'll probably get there about ten after twelve." It wouldn't do any good to ask Cherie why she wanted to meet. She would say, "If I wanted to talk about it over the phone, I would."

"See you then, dear."

Oh, she could sound so innocent. "See you then, dear,"

she'd said, as if she were a sweet old lady instead of the totally hip, high-energy, wise woman she was.

The morning flew by. There was little conversation between the staff, each person focused on their own work with a single-mindedness that Maureen hadn't seen before. No one had brought donuts or homemade goodies. No laughter rang in the air, just a steady hum of everyday office sounds—phones ringing, copiers, strictly business conversations.

The fresh air revitalized her when she left for lunch, taking a streetcar to the end of the line on Market. Cherie met her at the stop, then they walked to the park together. Known for its palm trees and cityscape view, Dolores Park was a great place to sunbathe and people watch. She and Cherie sat on a park bench and dug into lunch, Chinese chicken salad. Paired with a loaf of crunchy artisan bread, it was the perfect meal for a late June day in San Francisco as the sun chased away the marine layer.

Maureen lifted her face toward the brilliant rays. She wasn't holding her breath waiting for Cherie to tell her the purpose of her invitation, but she was curious. However, the longer Cherie delayed in bringing it up, the more curious Maureen got. Finally concern nudged curiosity aside. It must be bad for Cherie to avoid talking about it for so long.

"You invited me here for a reason," Maureen said, needing to get the conversation going.

Cherie nodded. "Your father called me yesterday."

"Ah. And how is Master Sergeant William Henry Hart?"

Cherie eyed her. "You know, dear, he's been retired from that position since you were fifteen."

"But the attitude lingers," Maureen said. "I remember his retirement well. The next day he married my second stepmother."

"A marriage that has stuck."

"What are you circling around?"

"Father's Day."

"What about it?" Maureen kept herself busy by putting lids back on the empty salad containers and wrapping up the bread.

"He hasn't heard from you."

"It was his choice to spend the day with his stepsons."

"True. And as it turned out, Riley had just arrived on your doorstep, so it worked out for you, as well."

"Right." She passed the shopping bag with the leftovers to her aunt.

"I think Bill is feeling hurt that you haven't arranged to have a belated Father's Day celebration. He'd love to see his great-grandson, too."

"The Bay Bridge goes both directions, Cherie."

"So do telephone lines," she snapped.

Maureen sat back in surprise. This was the purpose of the picnic? To chastise her about her father? "You're mad at *me*? He's the one who had other things to do on Father's Day."

"You know how he is."

"I do. And I've gotten tired of always being the one to do the inviting. Sometimes it would be nice for him to make the effort, you know? Anyway, with Riley here, I've been busy. I know I'm being selfish, but I don't feel a need to apologize for it, either. Dad had his chances, Cherie. With me *and* with Jess. If it hadn't been for you, I would've been living on the streets when Jess was born."

"That was a long time ago. And you know how he is," Cherie said again.

"I know I didn't live up to his expectations. I know I never made him proud. And still I've done my duty. I don't ignore Father's Day or Christmas or his birthday."

"Anyone can buy a present." Cherie's voice was a shaky whisper in the breeze.

The slightest bit of panic snaked through Maureen. "You've never pushed about him before."

"No, I haven't."

"Why now? Is he ill?"

"Not that I'm aware of."

"You? Are you ill?"

"I'm tired of being the intermediary between you two, Maureen."

"It's a role you've played since Mom died, then again through his divorce and yet again during my pregnancy, when he kicked me out. You've always been in the middle."

"Well, I want to be done with that. I'm seventy years old, and I've had enough."

"I understand you're tired of it. I just don't understand why you're pushing *now*."

"Everyone has a breaking point, dear."

Maureen sensed it was more than that. Cherie had been aunt/mother/counselor for all of Maureen's life. Any change in these roles had significance, but apparently Cherie wasn't saying why.

Maureen laid a hand on her aunt's, clasped in her lap. "I'll call him." She couldn't promise to do more than that. There was a lot of water under this particular bridge.

"He didn't kick you out, you know," Cherie said quietly.

Maureen went rigid. "Do we have to talk about this again?"

"We haven't talked about it in years. Yes, I think it's time to talk about it again. It's past time for you to see the whole picture. He did not kick you out, Maureen. You threatened to leave, and he didn't stop you."

"Doesn't that amount to the same thing?"

"Not in my book. He knew you would come to me for help. Knew you would be safe."

"He never once asked me to stay." She could hardly get the words out. "Never asked me to come back."

"Then when almost the same situation happened with your daughter, did you ask her to stay? Ask her to come back?"

She didn't even have to think about it. "Of course I did."

"Ask Jess what her impression was, and I'll bet you get a different answer."

"I did not abandon my daughter." Fury rose in Maureen, fast and hot. "And I stayed in touch. I would've swooped in at any moment if I thought she needed me to. I didn't let Daniel take on the whole financial load, but sent her clothes and gift certificates. I visited. I paid their way to fly here for visits. Don't you dare compare me to my father in that way. In *any* way."

"Bill didn't abandon you, either. You kept yourself from him, and he didn't know how to change it. It's much harder for a man, you know. That's why I admire Daniel."

"Why are you bringing Daniel into this? It has nothing to do with him."

"You need to think about that. After you have, we'll talk again." She glanced at her watch. "You're going to be late getting back to the office."

Maureen tried to focus on what she said. Late? For the office? Normally that wouldn't matter, but today, with all the pressure at work?

They walked to the streetcar stop. The relaxing picnic in the park had turned tense.

"I'm taking Riley to the ceramics shop tomorrow," Cherie said, channeling the discussion down a different path. "Then he and Daniel are doing my Mobile Meals run with me."

My father did abandon me. He did. "I'm sure he'll be thrilled. Riley, that is."

"Daniel asked to come along. Are you and he getting along better?"

"Most of the time." How could Cherie admire Daniel, when his actions had hurt Maureen so much?

But…there *was* a difference. Daniel had never tried to stop Maureen from moving to Seattle. She'd stopped herself. How long could she stay angry at Daniel when she'd actually been the one to deny herself?

"I'm glad you've found common ground," Cherie said. "I saw him Saturday. He seems to have settled in comfortably."

"What do you mean?"

"He was having dinner with a woman. A much younger woman, I might add. They were…cozy."

Ignoring the little internal jolt, Maureen focused on the streetcar headed toward their stop. "Did he see you?"

"I don't think so. I'm certain he would've said hello."

"Why didn't you approach him?"

"As I said, he looked cozy."

What did that mean? They were kissing? More than that? She couldn't say she was surprised. Even Riley had pointed out that Daniel had lots of girlfriends.

It struck her that maybe this was the purpose for Cherie's invitation—to talk about Daniel. Maybe the conversation about Maureen's father had just sort of happened.

She decided not to give Cherie the satisfaction of discussing Daniel, dropping the subject altogether as the streetcar arrived.

Maureen and Cherie boarded together, although Cherie would transfer in a few blocks to another bus to take her to the free clinic where she volunteered three afternoons a week.

"You haven't said a word about Ted," Cherie commented after they were seated.

"Nothing to report."

"Is he still handling everything okay?"

"He took us to a Giants game on Saturday."

Cherie held her gaze for a long time. "I wish I could see stars in your eyes when you talk about him."

Maureen felt her jaw tighten. "I saw stars once. The light obscured reality. He's a good man, Cherie. He'll stand by me."

"He's a good, dull man, and you've become a good, dull woman." She signaled that she wanted to get off at the next stop. "I'm sorry for being so blunt, but it's the truth. You're still a young woman. You should have stars in your eyes."

She left Maureen brooding for the rest of the bus ride. She'd been so happy to find Ted, a man with whom she had so much in common. Now she'd begun rethinking the relationship, and she didn't like that.

She banished the thoughts as she got back to her office. The quiet struck her again. Usually there was happy noise in the place.

As soon as she sat at her desk, Anza sneaked—there was no other word for it—into her office.

"You're late," Anza whispered.

"Five minutes. I was here five minutes early this morning. Was that noted?" She knew she sounded snippy, but she didn't like being put on the defensive. "And how many times have I eaten lunch at my desk in the past few months? All of us have done that and not complained."

Anza held up her hands in surrender. "You got a call from George Linninger's wife."

"His wife?" That couldn't be good news. George was one

of their premiere authors of the ShortTakes, their Shakespeare expert.

"He was in a car accident."

"How bad?"

"Broke his back."

"Oh, my God. Is he…" *Paralyzed?* She didn't even want
to imagine it.

"They're not sure of the prognosis as yet, but at the least
he's going to be laid up for a long time. They have to wait
for the swelling to go down before they even have an
inkling. Bernadette wants to know what he's got in the
pipeline."

Maureen opened her file on Linninger. "Two at the
printer. One on your desk for proofing." She looked at Anza
for confirmation.

"I'm working on it now, in fact."

"He's under contract for three more, and we expected to
use him until we were done with Shakespeare altogether.
He's supposed to have the next one turned in August fifteenth, so maybe he's well into it and someone can finish
it." Maureen pushed her hair away from her face and stared
at her desk. "Poor George. He's such a dream to work with,
too." She wondered how long they could reasonably wait
before they would have to make other plans.

She thought about George, wondering if he would walk
again. Her thoughts eased toward the pregnant Bonnie,
trying to take care of herself and her young daughter while
stuck in bed. Maureen's problems were insignificant in com-

parison. She knew Bonnie had daily help now, thanks to Cherie, but since Riley's arrival, Maureen had neglected the mother and daughter.

She spun her Rolodex until she found Bonnie's number. "Hi, it's Maureen."

"Hi! We missed you on Saturday, but Cherie told us all about your grandson and going to the Giants' game."

"I missed you, too. Cherie is going to take Riley with her tomorrow to meet you and Morgan. I was wondering if I could pick up Morgan for a playdate with Riley on Saturday?"

"She would love that! Thank you so much."

"I'm happy to do it. I'm sorry I've been out of touch."

"It's no problem."

"Yes, it is. And I intend to fix it."

"Well, okay, then. See you on Saturday."

Maureen hung up feeling much better. Now all she had to do was face Daniel.

CHAPTER 10

Rileyism #15: "But he's old. And I need *to see those pictures."*

Maureen opened her front door with anticipation and dread.

"Grandma's home!"

That cheerful, welcoming voice dispatched Maureen's anxiety as her grandson raced down the hall to greet her. She hugged him a little too hard and a little too long, she realized when he tried to wriggle free. Over his head she saw Daniel mosey toward her, wiping his hands on a kitchen towel.

Her stomach clenched.

Hunger pangs, she told herself, as an incredible smell filled the air. He'd cooked something wonderful again.

As he got closer, she stood and Riley ran off.

"Come watch *Animal Planet* with me, Grandma," he called as he rounded the corner into the living room.

"Why don't we let your grandma put down her stuff and change her clothes, bud?"

"O-kay." The word dragged with disappointment.

"You look like you could use a glass of wine," he said, flinging the dish towel over his shoulder.

I could use a hug. She took a step toward him then stopped. They hadn't broken eye contact since he'd first come into the hall.

He took her briefcase. "Rough day?"

"Things are tense at work. And my aunt gave me hell for something."

"One glass of merlot coming up."

She eased her head from side to side, trying to break up the tension settled in her shoulders that was transforming into a headache. It was nice coming home to someone who saw when she needed tending to.

"That would be great, thanks. I'll go change."

"Grandma! Come see. The girl lion's gonna kill dinner for the boy lion."

Maureen grimaced. Daniel grinned. "Bloodthirsty grandson we've got," he said.

"I can only hope the kill is done by the time I join him." Still, she didn't move but stood staring at Daniel, at his thick, shiny hair, his laughing eyes, his broad shoulders, which seemed to bear the weight of the world much better than her own. "Are you rushing off or having dinner with us?"

"I can stay for a while. No Ted tonight?"

Maureen realized she hadn't spoken to him all day, had barely thought of him, in fact. They hadn't ended things too badly last night. Why hadn't he called? Why hadn't she called him? "I don't know," she said to Daniel. "I should call and see what his plans are."

What she really wanted was a hassle-free evening, and Ted was bound to be annoyed that she hadn't gotten in touch with him at some point during the day—which she should have.

In her bedroom she changed into jeans and a T-shirt. She freshened her makeup and brushed her hair, spritzed a little perfume into the air and walked through it. Then she sat on the bed and called Ted but got no answer. Relieved, she joined Riley and Daniel in the living room.

"You missed it, Grandma. It was cool."

"What a shame." She pulled him into her arms for a big bear hug until he giggled. He'd gotten comfortable with her, and instigated hugs himself sometimes. Progress.

"Your wine's on the coffee table," Daniel said, smiling at Riley as he relaxed against Maureen.

"You're spoiling me." Not only had she never had anyone take care of her the way Daniel had since he'd come, she'd never taken care of anyone that way, either, except her daughter, which was entirely different. "What is that mouthwatering smell coming from the kitchen?"

"Lentil stew. We've got a coleslaw, too, with cabbage, carrots and peanuts."

"Yeah. Definitely spoiling me."

"And we made brownies," Riley said, stretching out on the floor with his cars, his usual position. "Peanut butter and chocolate."

"Maybe I should've worn something with an elastic waist."

"You could go for a walk after dinner," Daniel suggested innocently.

She sat on the sofa and picked up her wineglass. "Didn't you hear? I can't do that. Can't exercise at all. Not allowed."

His gaze went up and down her, as if looking for apparent incapacities or injuries, but he lingered here and there, making her heat up on the inside.

"Why not?" he asked.

"I'm in the Fitness Protection Program."

He laughed, the sound drowning out the television. Riley looked up with a broad, missing-front-teeth grin. Maureen smiled, too. She sipped her wine, relaxing finally, glad she'd decided to give up her anger, both at him and herself. Holding on to it was useless and exhausting. She wanted a clean slate. "How long until dinner's ready? Is there anything you need me to do?"

"Everything's done. Table's set. I'm giving the stew another fifteen minutes or so." He cocked his head, studying her. "Scoot yourself onto the floor. I'll give you a shoulder rub."

She took a sip of her wine as she debated his offer. She certainly wouldn't mind a shoulder rub, but to have his hands on her? She remembered how she felt trying to get the toy car out of his hair, how thick and tempting it was. And she had been in control then, not him. This time he would be in control.

But Riley's right here. What could happen?

Daniel leaned close. "Get your mind out of the gutter, Grandma."

She didn't like that he could read her that easily. But then, he'd had a lot of experience reading women.

She sat on the floor. He slipped behind her on the sofa and started working her muscles. Oh, yeah. He was good. She set her wine on the coffee table and closed her eyes, letting herself go limp as his hands worked magic.

"You don't relax enough," he said.

"Mmm."

"You're agreeing with me on something?"

"Don't get too cocky."

"Most women don't complain about that."

She could hear laughter in his voice, and his fingers stilled for a few seconds.

"Most women are aware of how fragile the male ego is," she said.

He laughed. "So you *do* have a sense of humor."

She didn't dare tell him she wasn't joking.

Riley pushed a tiny Corvette across the floor and up Daniel's leg. "Papa, come play with me."

"Can't, bud. I've got to finish dinner. I'm sure your grandma would love to."

At the dinner table a few minutes later, Riley regaled Maureen with tales of their day. Maureen had come to realize that Riley wasn't a fussy eater like most kids his age, although he did love sweets a lot. She could remember battles at the table with Jess, with dire threats made if she didn't eat at least three bites of everything.

What had Maureen been thinking, making mealtime a war zone instead of a place to connect? They'd been alone at the table. They could've talked as she and Riley were now—about what happened that day, observations about the world, plans for the future.

How many times had she dropped the ball when she'd had an opportunity to forge a stronger mother/daughter bond? No wonder Jess had rebelled so much.

A moment flashed in Maureen's mind of Jess at six or seven years old, telling Maureen she was going to live with her babysitter because *she* was *fun*.

It had hurt at the time, but she'd felt a strong obligation to raise her daughter to be a responsible human being.

What a horrible mother she'd been—

"Maureen?" Daniel's voice came quietly into her consciousness.

She flinched at the touch of his hand on hers.

"Everything okay?" he asked lightly, as if not to alarm Riley.

She saw worry in their grandson's eyes. He'd stopped shoveling food into his mouth, his fork suspended midair.

She smiled. "Just taking a trip down memory lane."

"Where's that, Grandma? Can you drive me there?"

"I can't drive you, but I can take you. We'll get out the photo albums tonight and I'll show you."

"Awesome!"

It had become Riley's assigned task to put the dirty dishes on the kitchen counter. Maureen and Daniel stayed seated at the table and finished their wine as Riley cleared things one by one, holding tight and taking slow steps.

"Do you want to talk?" Daniel asked.

"About what?"

"Your tense work environment? Why your aunt gave you hell? Why you didn't know whether Ted would be here tonight for dinner? Why I had apparently agreed to stay overnight with Riley last night, when, in fact, you'd never mentioned it? Why—"

"Whoa. How many questions do you think I can hold in my head at one time?"

"I figured if I asked enough questions you might actually answer one of them."

She smiled. Smart man. "Which one is the most important to you?"

"Why I was supposedly spending the night."

Maureen weighed her answer, waiting until Riley was in the kitchen. "Ted thought I was going to ask you to spend the night so that he and I could have some time alone."

"Together."

"Well, yes. Obviously."

"But you didn't call me. I dropped by."

"I didn't want to go."

"Why not?"

Riley ran back in and grabbed another plate, then walked cautiously away.

"It's not important," she said at last. *Because Ted was clinging. I don't like clinging.*

"Let me guess, then. Nothing else matters but Riley right now."

"Mostly, yes."

Daniel set his empty glass on the table. "In a month, when Jess returns, Riley will leave. That's a long time to ask your boyfriend to play second fiddle."

"Ted understands how important this is to me."

"No man understands taking a backseat for that long, Maureen."

Why did he feel it was his duty to give her unsolicited advice, especially something that would make Ted happy?

Riley came back for the silverware, moving around the table to pick up all the pieces, making a silver bouquet in his small hands, then leaving again.

Maureen turned to Daniel. "Since you shared your heart-breaking relationship with your son, I understand why having Riley so predominantly in your life is critical to you. Because of that, as well as sharing Riley while Jess is gone, we've gotten closer." She stopped, having lost her train of thought. "I have no idea where I was going with this," she admitted.

"I don't either, especially since what you just said has nothing to do with what I'd said before—that no man wants to play second fiddle."

"Now I remember. I wanted to say that just because we seem to be getting along better doesn't mean I want unsolicited advice from you."

"Even when it's right?" His eyes sparkled.

"Especially when it's right."

He laughed, then he pushed away from the table. "Hey, bud, I'm taking off."

Riley ran in and flung himself at Daniel. "I love you, Papa."

Daniel lifted him into his arms and touched foreheads. "Love you, too. I'll see you in the morning. Don't forget, we're going with your aunt Cherie tomorrow for her Tuesday rounds."

"I 'member. Do we get to eat the food, too?"

"Nope. It's special food. But she said we could take her for ice cream sundaes when we're done."

"Cool!"

"Yeah." Daniel planted a kiss on Riley's cheek then lowered him to the floor.

Fresh envy rushed through Maureen at their closeness. She was getting there with Riley, but she would never have their comfortable, openly loving relationship. Six weeks couldn't compete with six years. She swallowed against the lump in her throat.

As Riley went off to play with his cars, Maureen followed Daniel down the hall to the front door.

"Thank you very much for dinner. And the shoulder rub. And the sympathy." She found it was easy to be sincere with him finally, instead of pretending. They had a common cause—Riley. He was binding them in surprising ways.

"Any time."

She waited for him to leave. He put his hand on the

doorknob, but didn't open the door and then turned back toward her.

"I know you've been on your own for a long time, Maureen. Been there, done that," he said with a slight smile. "It makes one defensive, to say the least. You learn to hide what hurts. You learn to make it go away, in a sense, by ignoring it. It felt good to tell you about Josh. I'd be honored if you'd like to share with me what your life with Jess was like."

"I'll share."

"Good. I'd also like to know about her father, because although she never talks about him, I'm gathering he's alive." He brushed a hand down her hair. "I won't judge, I promise."

"I haven't even talked about him with Ted," she said, tempted to press her head against his palm, to take some kind of comfort as memories slammed into her.

He touched her chin, lifting her face a little. "If you can't share that sort of thing with him, it doesn't bode well for a solid relationship, does it, Maureen?"

On that note he left. He hadn't said anything she didn't already know and had acknowledged. It wasn't that she hadn't wanted to tell Ted. But he hadn't shared much about his past and hadn't wanted to hear about hers, as if the past had no bearing on now and the future. And maybe the shame of it all made her not force the issue. He'd given her an easy out.

Later that evening, after Riley was in bed, she pulled out the paperwork she'd brought home, but her attention was scattered. Too much crowded her mind. There was Riley and Jess, first and foremost. Cherie's reminder about her duties as a daughter, yet another issue. The promotion, her payoff for nineteen years of hard work. And Ted, a different kind of payoff, one that she had been thinking would last the rest of her life.

Daniel was a big complication. He was forcing her to analyze, something she didn't want to do. And to rethink her opinion of him.

We are all products of our parenting, she decided, good, bad or indifferent. Her conversation with Cherie echoed in her head long enough that she picked up the phone and dialed her father.

"Hi, Dad," she said as cheerfully as she could manage. "How are you?"

"Doin' well, Mo. Doin' well. What's up?"

"We missed Father's Day. I wanted to invite you to dinner on Sunday."

"Cherie opened her big mouth."

She counted to five. "Cherie realized I needed a little reminder because I've been overwhelmed with other things. Riley is here and work has been a zoo. It just slipped my mind. I would've remembered and called, Dad. Truly."

He made a sound that could've meant anything.

"So, can you come on Sunday?"

"Sure. You're inviting Norma, too?"

One-two-three-four-five. "Of course." Like she wouldn't invite her stepmother? They both needed the chatty Norma to be there, otherwise there was little conversation between father and daughter.

"Good. How's the boy?"

"A wonder."

"You hadn't figured on telling me he was there? I had to hear about it from Cherie?"

One-two-three-four-five. Six. Seven. "He'll be here for another month, Dad. I wasn't keeping him a secret. We had some settling in to do first."

They decided on a time to meet, then hung up. From the coffee table Maureen picked up the photo album she'd shown Riley—their trip down memory lane, photos of Jess growing up. He'd used the word *silly* about a hundred times, but Maureen could tell he enjoyed seeing his mom growing up, especially at age six, like him, with the missing front teeth.

Maureen ran her hand over one photo, letting her fingers drift along Jess's sweet little face. She'd missed her daughter so much, more than she'd admitted to anyone, more than she'd even admitted to herself, to keep from sinking into depression over the fact her only child had turned her back on her. Maureen had focused her already intense dedication to her job, filling up the empty hours, but always in the back of her mind expecting Jess to come home, bringing Riley with her.

She'd never believed they would stay away. Never. The grass is always greener, she'd thought. Jess would see that it wasn't any different living at Daniel's. But Maureen had been wrong. They hadn't come home. And it *had* been different living at Daniel's. He'd made their life a whole lot easier than Maureen could have—or would have. She did as much as she could long distance.

Maureen closed the album and her eyes. So many mistakes. So many missed opportunities. With her father, too? Had their estrangement been mostly her fault?

The photo album beneath her hands gave her strength. Memories of that smiling little girl and that darling grandson sleeping in her guest room told her everything she needed to know—she had to put the past behind and start a new relationship with her daughter. Maureen had been able to relax her usual rules and regulations with Riley, so she *was* capable of changing her ways. She could change her ways with Jess, too. They'd already missed out on too much in each other's lives.

She had to learn to relax, to play more, to go with the flow, as Cherie would say. She'd already made a start with Riley.

Maureen sighed at the irony of her conclusion—she needed to be more like Daniel, to find a way to be more flexible, more open to the adventure.

But she wasn't ever going to stop being punctual.

MAUREEN AND RILEY made the Mobile Meals rounds with Cherie on Saturday, as usual. Riley had already made friends with everyone on the route. He leaned against the arm of Arnold Konrad's wheelchair and talked with the eighty-six-year-old about African safaris, a discussion they'd started on Tuesday. Mr. Konrad had tracked down his photo albums of the safari he'd been on in 1949, when he was young and vital and had a full head of hair, which fascinated Riley. Maureen was only able to get him to leave by promising he could come again.

"But he's old," Riley protested. "He could die. And I *need* to see those pictures."

Mr. Konrad chuckled.

"I imagine your grandpa would be happy to bring you to visit again, if that's okay with you, Mr. Konrad."

"I'm not going anywhere," he said, gesturing to his wheelchair.

"Me and Papa could take you outside and push you around," Riley said.

"It's quite a steep hill I live on."

"Papa's very strong."

Maureen smiled. She loved how generous and caring her grandson was. And she was sure Daniel wouldn't mind the offer being made in his name. He was good at taking care of people, a fact that had stopped surprising Maureen, who was fairly certain that Riley had learned sympathy because of Daniel's easy kindness.

"That would be very nice," Mr. Konrad said, his voice wavering a little. "I don't get out much. Mostly just to see doctors." He hugged Riley, who grinned ear to ear.

"Your dinner's ready, Arnold," Cherie said, setting a plate, salad bowl, and a mug of hot tea on his dining table. She'd taken his blood pressure when they'd first arrived, plus made a general assessment of his health, as she did every time she came, with everyone on her route. Arnold

Konrad was a long-term client of Mobile Meals, whom Cherie met at the free clinic.

"See you real soon, Mr. K., " Riley said, waving goodbye.

Next they visited Matilda Jones who'd had hip replacement a couple of weeks ago. She would be on her own again in a week or so. Then Jefferson and Bessie Mae Palmer, married seventy years, both of them blind but determined to stay in their home, able to do so partly because of Cherie.

It was the first time Maureen had seen or spoken to her aunt since Monday when they'd had their talk in the park, and now they were tentative with each other in a way they hadn't been before.

"I called Dad," Maureen said to Cherie as they drove to their last stop, Bonnie's apartment. They weren't bringing meals anymore, since they'd gotten someone to help daily, but Cherie still dropped in to see her, and Maureen was going to take Morgan on a playdate with Riley.

"I heard."

"He's coming over tomorrow for a belated Father's Day barbecue."

"Good."

"Thanks for the prod."

"You're welcome."

"Want to join us?" Maureen asked hopefully.

Cherie laughed. "You know I spend my Sundays at the soup kitchen."

"I know, but…"

Cherie patted Maureen's arm. "It'll be fine. Norma's coming, right?"

"Yes. It's not being with him that bothers me. It's knowing what I know now, thanks to you. That maybe he didn't really kick me out. It puts a whole new spin on my relationship with him."

"As it should."

"Why didn't you tell me before?"

"You wouldn't have understood before. Now you do."

"Because of Jess?"

Cherie shrugged one shoulder. "More than just her. You'll figure it out."

"You're a puzzle, Auntie."

Cherie's eyes lit up. "Why, thank you, dear."

"Are we there yet?" Riley asked from the backseat.

"What's your hurry?" Maureen asked, glancing in her rearview mirror for a second.

He grinned. "I like Morgan."

Good grief. He was six years old and already thinking romance…

Something else Daniel had obviously passed on to his grandson.

CHAPTER 11

Rileyism #17: "A carrot is just a carrot."

Maureen's stomach clenched when she opened her front door to her father. Only her father. "Norma's not with you?" she asked.

"She wasn't feeling well."

Who was going to be their buffer? How many long, strained silences would they have to endure? She would need to keep music on in the background so that there was noise. Why, oh, why had Cherie had other plans? She would've helped fill the voids.

You'll be okay, she told herself. Riley wouldn't be shy. And Ted was there. Plus, Maureen's new goal was to be looser, not to worry so much, to ignore the past as much as possible. She gave her father a quick hug, startling him, making him stiffen at the gesture. She couldn't remember the last time they had hugged—or even touched. "Come in, Dad. Happy belated Father's Day."

Riley was filling up a car at his toy gas station when they entered the living room. Ted stood behind the sofa, but came forward and extended his hand. "Good to see you again, Bill."

"How are you?" her father replied.

"Very well, thank you, sir."

The men had met only once—at a small dinner party Maureen and Ted had thrown at Scoma's a couple of months ago to celebrate her father's birthday—but the men had the army in common, as Ted had spent four years in the service. It startled her to realize that he was only sixteen years younger than her father, who didn't show his age. He seemed as fit now at sixty-six as he was while he was still in the army, even during his drill-instructor years.

"Riley," Maureen said. "Come say hello to your great-grandpa." She hoped her father wouldn't criticize Riley for not getting to his feet instantly, as she had been taught to do when an elder entered a room. As Jess had been taught, too. But the world was more casual now and such manners didn't seem to apply anymore.

Riley shook his great-grandfather's hand, his expression serious. Over breakfast that morning, Maureen had explained who he was and what the relationship meant, and that he'd met his great-grandfather twice before, when he was very small, and that it was okay not to remember him.

"Here," Bill said, handing a shopping bag to Riley. "These are for you."

Riley's whole demeanor changed. "Thanks, Papa Great!"

Maureen noticed a ghost of a smile on her father's face

at the nickname. He hunkered down then to help Riley rip wrapping paper off the biggest box.

"It's an army tank! Awesome."

"It's got a remote control. It'll climb hills and go over rocks. Small ones, anyway."

"Can I play with it right now?" He fumbled with the box end, trying to open it.

"Yes, you can, young man. Your grandma's backyard will make a good course. But aren't you going to open the other present?"

Riley grinned then, and Maureen saw her father soften even more. If she hadn't seen it with her own eyes…

Riley peeled off the paper. "It's an army guy, Grandma. Look."

"G.I. Joe," Maureen said, memories flooding her. She'd had a few of those herself when she was growing up, gifts that she hadn't played with but put on her shelf with reverence. During her father's tour in Vietnam she'd had a ritual of kissing them good-night, God-blessing them to keep him safe. He'd been safe. It was her mother who'd died while he was away.

"That's a proud uniform he wears, son, understand?" her father said to Riley as they removed the action figure from the box.

Understand? It was the word she most associated with her father. That drill-sergeant word had peppered every conversation, was used in all different tones—soft, harsh, commanding, even sarcastic. She'd wanted to wipe the world free of the word.

Riley stared wide-eyed at his great-grandfather, somehow knowing the importance of the toy, that it represented something bigger than play. "I understand, Papa Great," he said solemnly.

Maureen wondered if Stripe would be replaced tonight.

"Let's go test out the tank," her father said, then sent a questioning look her way.

"Sure, that's fine. Dinner won't be ready for a little while."

Grandfather and grandson headed toward the kitchen and the back door. Ted lingered.

"That went well," he said.

"Amazingly well."

"See? He's not as bad as you think."

Yes and no. Her memories weren't totally skewed. *But* it was time to let go of all that old hurt—past time, if Cherie was right. Her fresh start, her need to be happier, meant getting rid of excess weight. She'd let her father's albatross of wrongs weigh too heavily for far too long.

"I'm going to join them," Ted said, then leaned close. "Frankly, I'm grateful his chatterbox wife didn't come. I'm amazed Bill tolerates her."

Tolerates her? Maureen thought as Ted ambled away. *Tolerates* her? What an odd thing to say. Norma filled up the quiet spaces in her father's life, something he must have wanted, because she'd been chatty forever. When she and her two young sons had come into her father's—and Maureen's—life, everything had changed. He'd married and retired from the Army at the same time. They'd moved from their last post in Fort Benning, Georgia, to Oakland, California, so that he could take a job as a warehouse supervisor, a place he now managed, even though he was past normal retirement age. He wouldn't know what to do in retirement.

At fifteen, Maureen had resented all of the changes that move had brought, but most of all she'd resented that Cherie had to leave to make room for Norma.

Riley came flying in. "Come see, Grandma. It's gonna be hecka fun!"

She followed him outside, then watched them build an obstacle course for the tank.

She stared at her father's back. She'd been so angry at him for so long. She'd also hurt him intentionally, retaliating for everything that had gone wrong in her life, starting with her mother's death, which hadn't been his fault, except that he hadn't been there. But a five-year-old little girl couldn't have sorted that out. She would only act out. Except that Maureen hadn't been allowed to do that, either. Her father would not stand for any misbehavior.

She watched him now, teaching his great-grandson how to man the controls to move the tank. He was extraordinarily patient with Riley, who was four years younger than the suggested age on the box. His expression serious, Riley concentrated on mastering the controls, even if his eye/hand coordination wasn't equal to the challenge yet.

Her gaze slid to Ted, hovering nearby, offering his own

opinions. She'd never seen him play before. The male-bonding moment was fascinating to watch. And yet...Ted was really just watching, not playing, she realized.

As Riley got the tank moving toward the pile of stones they'd built, they all got quiet. Then as the tank crawled over the pile, they cheered.

So did Maureen, joining them to high-five Riley.

She caught her father's gaze as he smiled at Riley. She couldn't remember him smiling at her that way, without expectation, unconditionally. Or maybe she'd conveniently forgotten how often he had. Maybe she'd been harder on him than he'd deserved.

"You want to try it, Grandma?" Riley asked, holding the controls toward her.

"You'll need to teach me how."

He puffed up, looking competent and pleased with his role as teacher.

And so the day passed. Ted barbecued chicken, marinated in his special concoction. Maureen made a potato salad, plus a tray of raw vegetables.

"How come you cut carrots in tiny pieces, Grandma?" Riley asked as they ate at the table outdoors and he held a julienned carrot aloft.

"I don't know. I just always have."

"You really don't remember?" her father asked.

"Should I?"

"Your mother cut them like that. After she died, you wouldn't eat them any other way. You said they tasted better."

"I don't remember. So, did you keep doing it that way?"

"Of course."

Of course, he'd said, as if he'd always been so accommodating.

"You're silly, Grandma. A carrot is just a carrot."

"I suppose so, sweetie." Unless it's also a touchstone. What else couldn't she remember? She actually had few childhood memories, none of them clear, as if pieces of dreams, not knowing where fantasy left off and reality began. She'd felt abandoned a lot, and was always expected to adapt to a constantly changing life—moving every two years, having two stepmothers, Cherie being sent away each time a new wife came along, the second one bringing two stepbrothers. Friendships that came and went with every move. New schools. It hadn't been easy.

It couldn't have been easy on her father, either.

She saw him chuckle at something Riley said. Maureen couldn't remember a happier day with her father. Even Ted seemed relaxed with Riley for the first time.

Her father caught her watching him then. He smiled, tentatively but directly. She reached across and laid her hand on his, then she stood to clear the dishes, leaving the men to lay siege against the rocks and dirt again.

It was a good day, she decided as she rinsed the plates, except something was missing. Two somethings—some*ones*. Jess would've put herself in the middle of the action. Daniel, too. She missed his easy laughter.

But it definitely was the start of something better.

CHAPTER 12

Rileyism #20: "It doesn't look like milk to me."

The best place in San Francisco to spend the Fourth of July was at Bernal Hill. From atop the hill, the various fireworks displays from the city were visible, as well as others across the Bay.

Staking their claim on a viewing space, Maureen, Ted and Riley laid blankets on the ground, then set out chairs and a cooler of traditional picnic food. Cherie would be along soon, bringing her contribution to the meal. Daniel was to join them, as well. Anza and Gabe, too.

Some of the neighborhood children were there, ones Riley had met at Holly Park, and he joined forces with them now, playing his new favorite game, Army. He'd gotten good at barking orders, repeating phrases his great-grandfather had taught him.

"Don't shoot till you see the whites of their eyes!" Riley bellowed.

Anza waved as she and her husband approached, hand in hand. She glowed, there was no other word for it. Her love for Gabe and her happiness over her pregnancy created a bright aura around her—around both of them, really.

"Gabe made a mocha-caramel cake," Anza said as they hugged. "Can we eat dessert first?"

"No rules today," Maureen said, giving Gabe a hug then directing him to where Ted was watching over their spot.

Gabe kissed his wife, patted her almost-flat belly and walked away, carrying their picnic gear.

"What a difference between your pregnancy and mine," Maureen said. "I wonder what it would've been like if…"

"If what?"

If Kirk had loved me, had married me, had wanted me. "If things had happened differently."

"Spilt milk, Maureen."

"I know."

Gabe didn't linger with Ted but hurried back to his pregnant wife. He was introduced to Riley and commandeered into being a private.

"He's going to be a good daddy," Maureen commented to Anza.

"One of the reasons I picked him. That's the advantage of getting married later in life, I think. You know exactly what you want. And he wanted children as much as I did."

Maureen hadn't known anything about Kirk, except that he'd wanted her, and she'd felt like she'd finally belonged somewhere, with someone. What a fool she'd been to have believed anything he'd said. He'd known exactly how to play to her weaknesses, exactly how to get what he wanted.

He'd dared her to break the rules, and she'd broken them gladly, anything to flaunt her independence in her father's face. Seventeen years old and she'd known everything.

Like mother, like daughter, too. Jess had been the same—except that she'd handled everything differently.

Anza laughed, pulling Maureen out of her memories. "Riley's got Gabe standing at attention."

Beyond where the kids were playing, Maureen spotted Daniel walking toward them, a woman at his side. More than that—holding hands. Her body language shouted that she was comfortable with him and flirting with him. And he was responding in kind.

Ted often held Maureen's hand in public but never more than that. Never a hug or kiss, not even a brief one. And they certainly didn't— "That's Sunny," she said, firing a surprised look at Anza. "You did set them up."

"No, I didn't, because you asked me not to. They found each other on their own. I told you they had a lot in common. I heard they met while running."

"Hey, Maureen," Sunny said when they met up. "I haven't seen you in ages. Since Anza's wedding, I think."

More important, since the wild bachelorette party the week before. Sunny had arranged for a stripper, then had done embarrassing things with him, even for a Rowdie.

Maureen's hope that Daniel might find someone he would move to San Francisco for—and therefore bring Jess and Riley back home—was predicated on the notion that the woman be someone much more appropriate than Sunny.

Really? a little voice in her head mocked. You'd be happy watching Daniel fall in love?

Gabe came over, but as introductions were made, Maureen realized Daniel hadn't said a word to her, had merely looked her straight in the eye, then, after a moment, nodded a greeting. She hadn't expected a hug—they never hugged—but he generally had some sort of jibe, something to tease her into a smile, a small flirtation that was part of his makeup. She supposed having Sunny there changed things, but it seemed more than that.

Why hadn't he even said hello?

As the time passed, Maureen tried to keep herself from looking with envy at Anza and Gabe. In the past she'd been able to shove aside any desire for having another child—except the brief moment when Anza had first announced her pregnancy. Maureen had never met anyone she'd considered marriage material until Ted, who didn't want children. And she certainly wouldn't have gotten pregnant out of wedlock again. Jess had been enough of a handful on her own, filling the remaining hours away from work to overflowing. There was no room for another child—or a husband. And there'd been so much guilt and shame associated with pregnancy for her. So much pressure.

But she watched Anza and Gabe, and saw that they eased things for each other. Gabe made the cake for the picnic. Anza remembered the jackets for the evening. Neither of them had to do everything. The baby would be a shared responsibility—and joy.

Maureen had been lucky to have Cherie to help shoulder the child-rearing load when Jess was little, but it was different from having a husband.

A husband. She'd studied Ted today, too. How he kept to himself, how he waited for others to engage him in conversation rather than initiating it. How he'd let her prepare and pack the picnic food, and toys for Riley, and the blankets. He'd helped to carry the items, but that was all.

It hadn't always been that way, but he seemed to be pulling back, making her feel guilty enough to do things to make him happy without his reciprocating—at the cost of her own happiness and contentment. Or perhaps he was being defensive, shielding himself from feeling left out of her life.

She'd thought she'd found a partner in Ted, but maybe she'd still been wearing the rose-colored glasses of infatuation and hadn't seen him clearly. Or maybe he'd been pretending and now the true Ted was being revealed.

Or was it the true Maureen who'd been revealed in the past few weeks? Who *was* she?

In some ways she had more of a partnership with Daniel, at least within the house. But watching him with Sunny now made her realize how limited the partnership was. He was becoming a friend finally. Since she didn't have to fight him for Riley's attention, she had relaxed, and she and Daniel had gotten easier with each other, but it wasn't the same as a partnership.

"You're lost in the clouds," Cherie said from beside her. They'd finished eating. The fireworks would begin soon.

Maureen hoped Riley would stay awake. He'd had an action-packed holiday.

"It's been a good day," Maureen said to her aunt, slipping an arm around her shoulders. "The last time I was here for the fireworks, Jess was about fourteen. After that she came with friends instead of me."

"To a teenager, Mom is always a stick-in-the-mud," Cherie said.

"I guess so. I hope she doesn't think so now."

"Children usually come to appreciate their parents. Speaking of which, I gathered from your father that things are better there, too."

It made Maureen happy that her father had felt it noteworthy enough to comment on it to Cherie.

"We're on track." Maureen looked toward where Daniel and Sunny were seated, Riley cuddled up next to his grandpa, pointing at the sky.

"It doesn't look like milk to me," Riley said before Daniel defined the Milky Way for his literal grandson.

Maureen bent toward Cherie. "Is Sunny the woman you saw with Daniel a while back in the restaurant?"

"Yes. Why?"

Because she wondered how long they'd been seeing each other. How serious a relationship they might have. Sunny rubbed her arms, as if cold. Daniel put his arm around her and drew her close. Maureen wished—

"Dear?" prompted Cherie.

"What? Oh, I was just curious."

"Look who I found." Ted came up with Bernadette, who looked different with her hair down and wearing jeans and a sweatshirt.

Cherie greeted Bernadette, then went off to join Riley, leaving Ted and Maureen alone with her boss.

"My family comes every year," Bernadette said, pointing toward where a large group were settling onto their blankets and into chairs to watch the show. A handful of children chased each other. A baby carrier held what must be Bernadette's newest grandchild, not even a month old. It was too dark now to sort out everyone.

"Looks like your gang's all here," Maureen said.

"Almost. Carlos Junior didn't come. He's with a new girlfriend."

"It seems strange having a day off in the middle of the week," Maureen commented.

"I went in this morning for a while," Bernadette admitted. "We need to talk first thing tomorrow about replacing George Linninger."

"No shoptalk," Ted said. "Maureen's working too much as it is."

Worried that Bernadette would think Maureen had been complaining, she immediately attempted damage control. "Everyone is working hard. This is an important time for Primero. Bernadette was also kind enough to let me take work home."

"We should've been in Paris today."

"We'll be in Paris in August."

Maureen knew that because Ted had known Bernadette for several years, he felt comfortable in saying things he would say to a friend. But Bernadette was her boss.

"Do you still plan to retire soon?" Bernadette asked him, which was news to Maureen. He'd never mentioned it. He was only fifty.

He actually looked a little sheepish. "Semiretire. I'm hoping to talk Maureen into it, too."

Shocked at his words—at the damage they could be doing to her potential promotion, possibly her entire career—she tried to smile, although she quaked with fury inside. "He's teasing, of course. He knows I have no intention of retiring. Not now, not anytime in the conceivable future."

"I'm glad to hear that," Bernadette said. "I should be getting back to my family. I'll see you in the morning, Maureen."

Maureen's heart pounded so hard she could barely hear. "How could you do that?" she asked Ted after Bernadette was safely out of earshot.

"Do what?"

"Sabotage my promotion like that." Was that it? Had it been intentional?

"You're being paranoid. I was making conversation."

"At my expense." How could she fix what he'd done? What did she need to say to Bernadette? "You implied I wasn't going to be staying on at Primero. What gives you the right to speak for me?"

"We've talked about retirement."

"Yes, retirement, in the broad sense of the word, as in age sixty-five. That's more than twenty-five years for me. I like my job." Her stomach churned. Nausea threatened.

"And I'll be seventy-five then. Long retired, certainly. Look, sweetheart, you've worked very hard all your life. Wouldn't you like to take it a little easier? And you've said many times how you'd like to see more of the world."

They weren't married—or even engaged. Why was he talking as if they were? "In the future. I'm nowhere near ready to retire."

"I don't see how what I said is so terrible." His voice had gone cold and tight.

"It's not your career on the line." She wanted to run over to Bernadette and fix everything right then. Sleep would be hard to come by otherwise.

"I was trying to do something nice for you."

"I—"

"The fireworks are starting," Ted interrupted, placing a hand at the small of her back, urging her toward their chairs.

And she'd thought she and Ted were alike, had been glad of it? It was scary to picture herself like him, paternal and patronizing.

Riley flitted back and forth between Maureen and Daniel as the displays lit up the sky at various points around the Bay.

During the height of the oohs and aahs, a thought struck her. If she could line up a replacement for George Linninger before she met with Bernadette in the morning, would that help her boss realize how dedicated Maureen was to her job?

As the fireworks ended and people packed up to leave, Maureen took Daniel aside. "I've got a proposition for you."

"I'm flattered. But as you can see, I'm with someone."

After a moment she laughed, which felt good after the stress of the past hour. "A business proposition."

"I never take payment for my services, excellent though they may be."

"And you're humble, too."

"When it's called for." He flashed a grin. "What's up?"

"Not tonight. How about coming about ten minutes early tomorrow morning?"

"Ahh. You're gonna make me wait. Make me wonder all night. There's a mean streak in you."

"Payback is hell."

He laughed then. "Touché. But just remember, you *perceived* I was an ogre all those years. Now you know differently."

"Daniel, I'm freezing." Sunny came up and wrapped her arms around him. He'd already given her his sweatshirt and was wearing a blanket over his shoulders. "Let's go do something to warm ourselves up," she murmured suggestively.

Daniel looked slightly embarrassed, or perhaps annoyed? "Do you need help with Riley?" he asked, gesturing toward where Riley lay, sound asleep, wrapped up tight in a quilt. He hadn't quite made it to the end of the fireworks before he'd dropped off.

"No, thanks. I've got everything under control." Unlike you, she thought, flashing a wicked grin at him.

He gave her a knock-that-off look in return, which made her smile even more.

"See you in the morning, then," he said.

"You certainly will."

An hour later Maureen slipped into bed, once again contemplating the unpredictability of her life. All she knew for sure was she was envious of Anza for being pregnant, angry at Ted for putting her on the spot with Bernadette, and jealous of Sunny.

She had to figure out which issue to deal with first.

CHAPTER 13

Rileyism #21: "I'm never gonna be bad ever again."

Maureen had tossed and turned most of the night, then overslept. She rushed to get ready for work, trying not to wake Riley, who still slept after the late night. She ran into the kitchen and grabbed a bagel to take with her.

"Do you know what those things do to your blood sugar?"

Maureen whirled. Daniel leaned against the doorjamb, his arms folded, a teasing glint in his eyes. He loved sneaking up on her.

She ignored the way her heart pounded, and chalked it up to the shock of finding him there. "When did you get here?"

"A few minutes ago. I waited in the living room. Didn't want to be accused of invading your privacy."

She grabbed a plastic bag and dropped her bagel into it. "You look like you ran here. Or maybe you just worked up a sweat with Sunny?"

"Jealous?"

"Get real."

"I'm as real as *True Grit*." He grinned. "Anyway, you should try it sometime. It's a great tension reliever."

"Sunny's not my type."

He laughed, low.

"Since *you* never seem tense, you must find relief a lot," she said, keeping things light.

"No comment." He pushed himself away from the doorway. "Seriously, Maureen. At least buy whole-wheat bagels. That one'll sit like a ball of raw dough in your stomach, abusing you for hours."

"It's my body to abuse."

"At least tell me you're going to put peanut butter or cream cheese on it."

"I'm going to put peanut butter or cream cheese on it." She smiled.

He shook his head. "So, what kind of proposition are you offering me?"

She pulled out a kitchen chair and gestured to him to join her at the table. "A situation has come up at work." She explained about their Shakespeare expert, who'd been injured in a car accident, and the problem that created for the ShortTakes releases to stay on schedule. "I'm wondering if you would be interested in the job."

"You're joking."

She'd been prepared for the fact he wouldn't be flattered by her invitation. "I know how you feel about what you call cheat sheets. I wouldn't ask if I weren't desperate."

"Why?"

"It's coming down to the wire for my promotion. I need to do something that puts me out front, that makes me shine."

He seemed to consider her words for quite a while. "I'd like to help you out, Maureen, but it would have impact on my reputation to associate myself. I've worked hard to get where I am."

"No author's name is attached to the ShortTakes. And your credentials are the same as Mr. Linninger's, by the way. He didn't have a problem with it."

"Linninger? As in George?"

"You know him?"

Daniel snorted. "Know him? We're like Tweedledee and Tweedledum when it comes to Shakespeare. George has published four books on the Bard, and I've done three. I'm also ten years younger, so I expect to pass him at some point. I can't believe he'd sink that low."

"We're providing a service, Daniel. A respectable service." She curled her hands into fists as she felt the door shut on her promotion. "If you don't see it that way, maybe you can recommend someone who might be interested?"

He hesitated. "I'll think about it."

"Can you think about it now? I don't have any time to waste."

"Just because you're ticked at Ted, don't take it out on me," he said.

A chill swept through her at the coolness in his voice. "Why do you think I'm ticked at Ted?"

"Come on, Maureen. You hardly acknowledged each

other last night, then after you spoke with your boss, you were firing daggers at Ted."

"Things were…tense, I admit. It'll pass."

He didn't reply for several seconds. "Is your job really on the line over this?"

Hope roared through her. "Not my job but my promotion."

"No exaggeration?"

"Do you think it was easy to ask a favor from you, of all people?"

His silence lasted more than a few beats. "All right, I'll fill in. But tell George that I'll back away as soon as he's ready."

She reached across the table and covered his hand with hers, relief flooding her. She didn't try to hide her gratitude. "I don't know how to thank you."

"Yes, you do."

She held her breath, waiting.

"Don't eat that bagel."

Her laugh was shaky. She stood, needing to get to work. Making a point, she left her bagel on the table, making sure he noticed.

"Bring me copies of what he's done so far, okay?" he asked.

"Hi, Papa. Hi, Grandma." Sleepy-eyed, Riley stood in the doorway, his G.I. Joe, named G.I. Bill after his Papa Great, dangling from one hand.

Good mornings and goodbyes were said. Maureen headed down the hall to the front door.

"Hang on a sec," Daniel said, catching up to her. He passed her a paper bag bearing the psychedelic logo of the PeaceLove Café. "The most important meal of the day."

"But…what will you eat?"

"Riley and I will go out for breakfast. He likes that."

"What delights am I having this morning?" She feared the worst—tofu, maybe. Or, even worse, soy bacon. She shuddered at the thought.

"Tomato and artichoke frittata, grapes and cantaloupe. Fresh-squeezed OJ."

She wanted to hug him. It must have shown in her face because he singsonged, "Thank you, Daniel. You're welcome, Maureen. Yada, yada, yada." He grinned. "Better get going. You don't want to be late today, of all days, Double-D."

He couldn't leave well enough alone, after all, but needed the last word to be a jibe.

She didn't want to give him the satisfaction of seeing her react to his teasing. "So, you and Sunny, hmm?"

He crossed his arms. "You got a problem with that?"

"No."

"Liar."

She bristled. "I was just curious."

"Liar." He moved closer. "You spent more time watching me last night than Ted."

"I did not." Had she? Was he right?

"Might as well face it, Maureen. You've got the hots for me."

She went rigid. "I do not have—"

"And I've got the hots for you. Been that way since the day I met you, more than six years ago. Why do you think we've fought so much?"

Lightning bolts zapped her erogenous zones at his words, then played a clamorous symphony. "Because you *stole* my daughter and grandson."

"Nope. Although that's part of it. It's chemistry, Double-D. Big-time, never-flagging chemistry."

"Not for me."

He smiled slowly, sexily. "Liar."

She shook her head. She'd heard about humans spontaneously combusting. She felt as if she could. "I *have* a boyfriend."

"In title only, I think. What do you see in him, anyway? He acts more like a father to you—or a teacher. I can only imagine what your love life is like. Do you ever get to take the lead? Be the instigator? Have you ever even been satisfied?"

That jarred her. "Of course I have."

"Baby, I don't think you have a clue what it means to be satisfied."

"Papa! Come quick. The bears are coming out of hibernation."

"We should continue this discussion another time," Daniel said to Maureen, his gaze direct.

"No," she said. "No." She left the house, trying not to hurry, trying not to show how much his words affected her.

Because he was right about way too much of it.

BERNADETTE WAS THRILLED that Maureen had found someone so highly qualified. They sat in her boss's office and chitchatted for a while, as in the old days.

"Something's different with your hair," Maureen commented. "I noticed it yesterday at the fireworks."

Bernadette tossed her head a little. "A combination of dark medium brown number fifty-two and dark brown number forty-six, to be exact. No more gray."

That was it—no gray. She looked brighter and younger.

Bernadette eyed Maureen's red hair, undoubtedly seeing the gray strands here and there, which had dulled the natural color. "You haven't taken the plunge yet, I see."

"No, although my hairdresser's been rubbing his hands about it, muttering something about virgin hair." Maureen grinned. "I'm scared to try."

"It's just hair. It'll grow back."

They both laughed at that absurdity.

Maureen felt cautiously optimistic at the conversation. She had wanted to ease into making sure her boss understood that Ted didn't speak for her when he talked about retiring. Now or never, she decided.

She leaned forward. "I want to reiterate to you that I'm not in any danger of leaving the company. I have no idea why Ted thought I might."

"I saw the shock on your face. But maybe you should consider it, Maureen. He's offering you something a lot of women would give anything to have. Travel, to be taken care of, financial stability."

"I love my job."

"That came through loud and clear."

Maureen took her cue. The discussion was over. Bernadette seemed a little annoyed with her, as if Maureen hadn't given her credit for having the insight to see what was obvious.

"Good. I'll gather the information for Daniel."

"Have Anza read the first draft of his work on *Twelfth Night*. She'll know if he's got the knack. Not everyone can do that kind of analyzing and condensing of material well."

Maureen was glad Daniel wasn't there to hear that. He might have quit at the implication he wasn't the best in the business. "Yes, of course. I'll keep in touch about it."

Maureen felt marginally better. She'd no sooner sat at her chair when her phone rang. Ted's name flashed on the tiny screen. She wanted to ignore it but didn't.

"Good morning," she said.

"Is it?" he asked.

She really didn't want to play games with him. "What do you mean?"

"Am I forgiven for butting into your business last night? For presuming something without talking to you about it first? I was an idiot."

In the past Maureen would've accepted his apology and—

Hold on. *Had* he apologized? No. He hadn't.

She straightened in her chair. She needed to stop being the peacekeeper all the time.

The good girl.

"You may have cost me my promotion, Ted."

There was a long pause. "It can't be as bad as that."

She said nothing.

"Let me make it up to you," he coaxed. "I'll call Daniel, ask him to stay with Riley tonight. We can spend some time together. That'll help. We just haven't spent enough time together lately."

She knew what he meant by "time." Just how would their having sex help fix things with Bernadette? she wondered. "I can't tonight." She explained about Daniel stepping in to help Primero out of a jam. "I have to review all the work with him."

"Let Anza do it."

"This is my job, Ted. I'm the author liaison. It's what I do."

"So, he should come in during business hours and talk to you."

"Would you watch Riley then, so he can?" When he didn't reply, she said, "Under normal circumstances I would do it that way. These aren't normal circumstances."

"So, the upshot is that I don't see you alone for yet another night. That makes almost three weeks, Maureen."

Petulance coated his words. While she understood his frustration, she didn't like how he handled it. Then again, she wasn't going out of her way to ease his frustration, either. He had reason to be upset about that. He'd had to make all the adjustments.

Maybe he, too, saw she was attracted to Daniel. There. She admitted it, at least to herself.

"We'll figure something out," she said, not knowing

exactly what, but believing what Daniel had told her about no man being patient enough to wait out six weeks. "I really need to get to work."

"Okay. Bye, sweetheart."

Maureen's day refused to fly by, even though she was busy. She watched the clock in anticipation of going home, the anticipation this time more about Daniel than Riley. The way Daniel had looked at her this morning still pierced her. She'd recognized there was attraction, of course, but it hadn't translated into "the hots," as he'd termed it. But now that he *had* termed it, she couldn't think of anything else.

She found distraction in arranging for Daniel's contract. She talked to George Linninger's wife and told her about Daniel stepping in temporarily, which seemed like a big relief to her.

Before Maureen left for home, she gathered information and samples for Daniel. Would he be too busy working to have time for Sunny? The thought had crossed her mind more than once during the day. She wasn't proud of herself for it.

Maureen was excited about going home—and felt guilty about being excited. And foolish, too. So they were attracted to each other. It wasn't the attraction that mattered, but what they did about it. That was what being an adult meant—controlling your impulses.

Riley stood in the front window, waiting for her. He grinned and waved, then disappeared, and she knew he would be at the front door the moment she opened it. Had

Jess done that, waited for her? She couldn't remember. She only remembered the distance between them when Jess was a teenager, not their closeness in earlier years.

You did the best you could.

It had become her mantra lately, reminding herself that she *had* done all she was capable of doing, given her own upbringing, circumstances and limitations. She was trying to forgive herself for however she'd messed up Jess's life by letting herself become like her father—or how she'd perceived him, anyway.

Riley charged her at the door, giggling and bouncing.

"What'd you do today, young man? Eat ten candy bars or something?"

"That's silly, Grandma." He grabbed her briefcase and carried it down the hall, the weight of it making him move awkwardly, but proud of himself for helping. "Papa and I went to jail."

"What?"

"I was in a cell an' everything. It was *awful*. I'm never gonna be bad ever again."

Maureen heard Daniel's footsteps. She didn't want to look at him, now that she'd been honest with herself about her attraction, so she kept her focus on Riley. "What did you do to land you in the hoosegow?"

"Hoosegow? That's not where we went. We went on a boat, Grandma. Just like me an' you did."

"Except we got off at Alcatraz," Daniel said.

"Tell Grandma we didn't go to a hoosegow, Papa."

They moved into the living room. "I think Grandma understands."

"Oh. Okay. Can I watch *Animal Planet?*"

"Just until dinner." Maureen picked up the remote. The picture came on just as a lion was devouring a zebra. She looked away.

"Which reminds me," Daniel said. "We're having tofu burgers for dinner."

Maureen smiled, but he didn't smile back. In fact, he'd barely looked her in the eye, much less indicated a shift in his feelings after their conversation that morning. Would they talk about it later?

The phone rang.

"If that's Ted, there's enough for him, too," Daniel said, then disappeared into the kitchen, sounding almost relieved to escape.

It was okay with him if Ted came over? Confused, Maureen picked up the phone and said hello.

"Bonnie's in labor," Cherie said abruptly. "I've called an ambulance, and I'm going with her to the hospital. Morgan would like to stay with you and Riley. Would that be okay?"

"Of course. I'll head right over."

Maureen approached Daniel in the kitchen. He wasn't doing anything but staring out the window over her sink into the backyard. She told him what was happening. "Can you stay with Riley until I get back or should I take him along?"

"I'll stay."

"Daniel?"

She wasn't wrong. He had retreated from her, but why? And how far?

"You'd better go," he said.

"If Ted calls—"

"I'll invite him for dinner."

She shook her head. "He won't want to be around two children. Just tell him I'll call him back, please."

By the time she'd picked up Morgan, had dinner, played with both children, read stories, then put them both to bed, the evening was gone—and so was Daniel. Without answers.

After Cherie called to say Bonnie had delivered a healthy boy, Maureen poured herself a glass of wine and sat at the kitchen table. So, Daniel was going to ignore their discussion about each of them having "the hots" for each other. Why?

And why should she encourage him to talk about it, anyway? She had Ted....

She took a swig of her wine then glanced at her wall calendar, where Riley had been marking Xs to know how many days until he reached the double-X at the end, marking his mother's return. Maureen didn't need Xs to know how many days remained. She was aware every second of the passing of time.

Especially on a day like this one.

CHAPTER 14

Rileyism #46: "So, now I hafta call you Mom."

Days flew, turning into weeks gone by. If Maureen was aware of every passing day, Ted seemed even more aware, reminding her daily like a countdown clock, and in the past few days asking her if she'd started packing for their vacation yet.

Her life was status quo. Ted's patience amazed her, especially since she hadn't made any effort to spend time alone with him. She and Daniel got along fine, but there were no conversations similar to the one weeks ago. It was as if it had never taken place. Everyone seemed to be biding their time. Even Bernadette hadn't decided who would be the new vice president.

And yet Maureen was happy, even content. She could let Riley go when it was time. Their relationship was solid and loving now, maybe not everything that he had with Daniel, but good enough.

At noon on a Saturday, six weeks minus one day after Jess had taken off, leaving Riley behind, she showed up, again without warning, two days earlier than they expected.

Maureen hardly recognized her daughter, who flung herself into her mother's arms and squeezed the breath out of her.

"Jess, honey." Maureen angled back, not letting go but needing to inspect her. "You've lost weight."

"And gained muscle." Utter happiness shone on her face.

"Your hair is almost white."

"Being in water and sun all day'll do that to a blonde."

"Are you well? Did you get hurt?"

"Sure, lots of times. But nothing major."

"Was it worth it, honey?"

"Oh, Mom. I can't tell you. I'm a different person."

"In what way?"

"I'll tell you later, okay? First I need to see my son. Where is he?"

"In the backyard." She followed Jess, who raced through the house, in time to see them embrace. Jess cried. Riley didn't seem to know what to make of her.

"Mommy?" he said finally. "I can't breathe."

Jess spun him around in circles. "Oh, I missed you, bud. I missed you soooo much."

"I missed you, too."

"Did you have a good time with Grandma?"

He nodded. "And Papa, too."

"Papa?" Jess set Riley on the ground. She sent a questioning look at Maureen.

"Daniel arrived the day you left. And stayed."

"Here?"

"No. We'll talk about it later." She rubbed Riley's back

as he snuggled against his mother. "I can't tell you how much this time has meant to me, Jess."

"I think I know. Mom, I have a lot to tell you, too, but first, there's someone I want you to meet."

Still full of surprises, Maureen thought, sighing inwardly. Noting the stars in Jess's eyes, Maureen knew the someone had to be male—and special. Stars in her eyes. It reminded her of Cherie talking to her about that very thing—that Maureen should have stars in her eyes. She hadn't realized what a barometer to happiness that was.

"Someone?" Maureen asked.

"His name is Keith Johansen. He's a consultant on *True Grit*. He's waiting outside."

"Did you win a bazillion dollars, Mommy?"

"Remember I told you it would be a secret for a while? Mommy signed a paper saying she wouldn't tell anyone until it's on TV."

"Even me?"

"Even you, sweet boy." She touched noses with him. "So, you had fun with Grandma and Papa, hmm?"

"Lots and lots. And Papa Great. And Auntie Cherie."

Jess raised her brows at Maureen. "Grandpa Bill? Looks like we *do* have lots to discuss."

"Why don't you invite your friend inside, honey." This man, Keith, had to be important to Jess. She'd rarely talked about a man since she left home, much less brought one to be introduced.

Maureen decided Keith must be around thirty. He was

as blond as Jess, with friendly blue eyes. He wasn't too tall, but obviously worked out, and more obviously adored Jess and vice versa. They didn't touch each other, probably because of Riley, but their eyes did, constantly, warmly, tenderly.

After an hour or so of clinging to his mother, Riley relaxed and began to build a new city with his cars. Keith joined him. Maureen and Jess went into the kitchen and sat at the table.

"You're in love," Maureen said.

Jess nodded. "He's amazing, Mom. I'm so lucky."

"So is he. You're pretty amazing yourself."

"Six weeks ago I wouldn't have believed that. I would've thought it was just my mom saying things moms say."

"And now?"

"Now I know what I'm capable of and who I am. I know that sounds cliché…"

"Not at all." Maureen rested her hand on her daughter's. "What are your plans now?"

"Keith and I haven't really had time together, but I couldn't wait to see Riley, so we drove straight here. We're going to take him and go somewhere, see if things work okay away from the unreality of the past six weeks."

"Yet you already know you're in love."

"It's wild, Mom. We were never alone with each other. We didn't even have a whole lot of time to talk, but we knew, you know? We both just knew. Do you think I'm crazy?"

Still her impulsive Jess, but in a different way, Maureen thought.

"Love *is* a little crazy, honey." Was that what was wrong with her relationship with Ted? It wasn't crazy? It had always been a sure thing, solid and steady. She'd liked that, had thought that was a good thing, but now, seeing her daughter's happiness…

"Can you stay overnight?" Maureen asked. "I'll invite everyone here for a party tomorrow. Your grandfather, in particular, would love to see you."

"I'd like to see him, too. Mom?"

"What, honey?"

"Something happened to me while I was doing the show. I'm not sure how to describe it, but many of us felt it, talked about it. It's a kind of spirituality, a oneness with the world. It's like we've been tested to the limits, and we not only survived, we became better and stronger, and yet more in touch with people and nature. I learned to love myself." She grabbed both of Maureen's hands. "I realized what a brat I've been. How much you sacrificed for me. I'm so sorry for all I did to hurt you. I know now that taking Riley away was cruel."

Maureen didn't try to stop the tears. "Oh, honey. I'm the one who needs to apologize. I had realizations, too, while you were gone. I was too strict with you, expected too much. I raised you like Grandpa raised me, even though I'd always resented him for that. I hope you can forgive me."

"If you can forgive me."

They fell into each other's arms. Could it be this simple? Maureen wondered. Could they bury the past that easily?

After a while they dried their eyes and returned to the

living room. Riley was straddled on Keith's back, driving a Hot Wheel up his spine and into his hair, as he had done to Daniel all those weeks ago. Keith's hair was much shorter, however, and the car didn't get caught. Riley grinned at Jess, then so did Keith.

"Mommy! I made you a present." He ran off to his bedroom, returning with a wrapped box. It was obvious he'd done the wrapping, which made it all the more special.

"For me?" Jess asked.

"Uh-huh."

He'd made her an I-Love-You plate, almost an exact duplicate of the one Jess had made for Maureen all those years ago.

"It's your special cookie plate, just like Grandma's. It says 'I Love You, Mom.' I wanted to put Mommy, but Auntie Cherie said my grown-up me would like it better if I put Mom. So, now I hafta call you Mom, 'cause I'm all grown up."

"Not yet, buddy boy," she said pulling him to her. "You're still my baby."

"Aw, Mom." He giggled. "I mean, Mommy."

The painting was less precise, since he was six and Jess had been twelve, but genuine emotion was embedded in the effort.

Six weeks ago Maureen never would have predicted how things would turn out, how her relationship with her daughter would change, but change it had. Everything had changed.

Whether it was all for the better, she just didn't know yet.

THE FOLLOWING DAY Maureen's house teemed with people. What had started as a small family event had expanded to

include Jess, Keith and Riley, Daniel, Cherie, Bill and
Norma, Norma's sons and their wives and children, Anza
and Gabe, and Ted—eighteen people. Maureen gave up
control and let others help by bringing food, without her
even assigning categories, a true potluck. They ended up
having more desserts than salads, but no one complained.

Her father had taken Riley for outings twice, cementing
their bond. Maureen had never seen her father smile so
much as when he was with Riley.

As the afternoon faded and people said their goodbyes,
Maureen took her father aside. She wanted to rid herself of
the final burden she carried.

"Dad, I realized recently that I never apologized to you
for getting pregnant. I know it embarrassed and hurt you. I
am sorry for that."

He looked around, whether in hopes of being rescued or
to make sure they weren't overheard, she wasn't sure.

"Water under the bridge," he said finally.

"No. It's water that's been dammed up. I resented you.
A lot. I wanted someone different from who you were.
What you were. I hated the Army. I hated the way we had
to move all the time. I hated that you were gone when Mom
died. I hated my stepmothers, although it was more that I
was angry because each time you married it meant Cherie
would have to leave, and I loved Cherie."

"I was trying to give you a mother."

"I see that now. It wasn't clear then. I especially hated
your two years as a drill instructor because you worked such

long hours. You were rarely home, and when you were, you were different, more rigid, if that was possible, more closed up. Cherie told me I should be grateful because at least you were home, not deployed, but I didn't care about that. I didn't like you then."

"Why are we having to talk about this?"

"Because I'm wiping all my slates clean. I need to. I want to live my life differently, more flexibly. I want to be happier than I am. So I'm asking your forgiveness for not being a very good daughter."

"You don't have to ask, Mo." He finally looked directly at her. He seemed to soften in a way she'd never seen before. "It looks like I'm the one who needs to ask forgiveness. After your mother died, I tried. I really did. But she was the good parent, not me. I could face the Viet Cong with less fear than I could my own daughter. I did retire from the Army rather than extending so that you could go to the same high school until you graduated."

"I didn't know that, Dad. I just assumed you'd put in your twenty years and were done with it."

"I wouldn't have minded going on. It was what I knew, what I felt comfortable with. I did the best I could for you, Mo."

I did the best I could. Maybe she and her father weren't too different, after all.

"I'm sorry, Dad." She wrapped her arms around him, then felt his encircle her. He was unfamiliar to her, they'd hugged so little during their lives. "I love you. I know I've had a strange way of showing it."

He moved her back a little but held her by the shoulders. "I love you, too."

Riley charged them, wrapping his arms around their hips and grinning at them. "Papa Great, come on. We need you. My cousins and I want to play Ten Hut."

"Seems I can't stop being a drill instructor, even to my grandchildren," he said to Maureen as Riley pulled him along to play the Hart family version of Simon Says. "Thank you," he said to her.

She nodded, a lump in her throat. She was free, and it felt wonderful.

Ted wandered over, a smile on his face. "Looks like you've settled things with your father."

"Yes. It feels good."

"And tomorrow Riley will be gone, and life can get back to normal."

What was normal anymore? Maureen wondered. Life seemed so different to her now, even though she had the same job, the same boyfriend, the same house.

"The new normal," she said. But he didn't respond to what she thought might open a conversation with him. Maybe he was afraid of her answers.

Maybe she was, too.

THE DISHES WERE PUT AWAY, the furniture returned to order. The only people left were Maureen, Jess, Keith, Riley and Daniel, who had Riley in his lap and was reading him a bedtime story. Riley's pirate-printed pajamas were the perfect accessory for hearing the particular chapter of *Peter Pan* that Daniel was reading.

"Are you gonna drive home with Mommy and Keith and me?" Riley asked when Daniel set the book aside.

"We're not going straight home," Jess said. "We're going to take a trip somewhere first."

"Where?"

"We haven't decided yet, bud. But someplace fun."

"I don't wanna go on a trip. I wanna go home..I wanna see Willy."

"You'll see him soon."

"I wanna go home with Papa."

"I'm staying here for a while longer, bud. I've got work to finish up for Grandma's company."

"Okay, young man," Jess said, standing. "Bedtime for you. Hugs and kisses to everyone."

An idea had been brewing in Maureen's head all afternoon. She followed Jess to the bedroom, then took her into the kitchen.

"I know you've missed Riley like crazy, Jess, but I've been thinking a lot about you and Keith taking him along with you. I don't think having a six-year-old is exactly conducive to you and Keith getting to know each other, do you?"

"Riley is the biggest part of my life, Mom. Keith understands that."

"I'm sure he does, and they're already off to a good start. How about this? What if you leave Riley here for a while longer, while you and Keith get things figured out. Maybe

Riley shouldn't get too attached to Keith until you know for sure that you have a future together."

"I hadn't thought of that. But, Mom, how can I leave Riley? He's going to have a fit. I just got back."

Maureen had always had some excuse, too, whenever Cherie had offered to keep Jess so that Maureen could take a vacation with the man she was dating. She'd always refused the generous offers, which she realized now had been a mistake. She'd been so proud, so insistent on succeeding on her own.

"I can take time off from work, vacation time. He's had a lot of time with Daniel, but not just with me. I think we can convince him he would have fun." It was something she should have done when he first came, she realized.

"But what about your Europe vacation? What about Ted, Mom?"

"Don't worry about that. This is what's important now."

"It's an incredible offer." She grinned. "I have to admit I'd like time with just Keith. We haven't even had sex yet!"

Maureen made herself not react. "Well, it's kind of hard to do that with a child around."

"If you're sure."

Maureen hugged her. "Never more sure of anything." Even though it was bound to change everything.

Everything.

CHAPTER 15

Rileyism #47: "Does Grandma have something wrong with her face?"

Riley was surprisingly okay with letting his mother go and to be left with Maureen. Maybe it was a comfort thing for a six-year-old, who'd gotten used to being somewhere and didn't want change. Maybe their relationship had just grown that much.

Whatever the reason, Maureen reveled in it.

Because there were repercussions to her offer to Jess, Maureen needed time to think about what came next. She offered Jess and Keith her house for the day so that they could be with Riley before they took off in the morning, then she got in her car and drove across the Golden Gate Bridge to the Marin headlands, her favorite place in the world to think.

Most of Maureen's big decisions had come while she sat on the ground looking at the bridge and the Bay and the city from high atop the hill. The wind blew her hair away from her face. She'd confronted reality here, many times—

the day she'd learned she was pregnant, the day she'd told the father of her child that he would become a daddy, the day she'd learned Jess was pregnant—and many others. It was her personal, silent sounding board. She usually left having made a big decision. Today would be no different.

As she sat staring at the vista, her tension ebbed, as if she were lying on a blow-up mattress with a slow leak. Her future had been set. Now it wasn't. Yet she felt good about the unknowns instead of worrying as she usually did. She was the Queen of Fret, a nickname Anza had bestowed on her years ago, with good reason.

Maureen finally headed back to the city, to Ted's house, the last stop on the unhappiness train.

"Well, this is a nice surprise," he said. "Come in. I guess your daughter has hit the road."

"They're staying until tomorrow morning."

"And you're here? I'm honored." He reached for her.

"Ted."

Her tone of voice stopped him.

"I told Jess that I would keep Riley while she and Keith spend some time together."

He mulled that over. "Okay. One more week of the status quo. As long as they're back by next Saturday when we leave. Or you let Daniel have him."

"I'm going to take my two-week vacation starting tomorrow. I want to spend concentrated time with Riley, not just three hours in the evening. I need to do that."

"You've had weekends."

It was true. She had, but she'd often had to share the time with Ted, so that she could keep him happy, too. She was tired of doing things to make everyone else happy.

"So," he said when she didn't respond. "You seem to have made some life decisions here without making me part of the discussion. You're canceling the vacation, obviously. Apparently it's the kid or me, and I guess the kid won."

"I won, Ted. *I* won. I've been increasingly unhappy. And I know I'm not making *you* happy, either." She pulled his house key out of her pocket and held it out. "I'm truly sorry, but it's better to know now than later."

He didn't take it, so she set it on a table.

"You're right, Maureen. I haven't been happy, but I was patient and, I think, quite generous in the way I handled having to deal with your sudden need to be a grandmother. You could've shared your attentions between Riley and me, but you chose to focus on him. You even gave up the Rowdies, something you never did for me. That told me a lot. The handwriting was on the wall when you refused to let Daniel keep him while we went on our long-planned trip. I should've walked away then."

"I'm sorry, Ted."

He cocked his head. "You know, I don't think you are. Not really. I think you're going to celebrate your freedom now."

"You're wrong. It wasn't an easy thing for me to do. I certainly didn't want to hurt you. I'm truly sorry that I have."

"Guess what?" he continued, his voice harsh. "I'm okay

with it. In fact, I plan to celebrate. I'm taking that trip. I've even got someone who'll go with me, someone who finds me attractive and a damned good catch."

His defensive tone made it easier to leave, although still stinging some. "I hope you have a great trip," Maureen said, then headed toward the door, realizing at the same time why she'd never lived with him—or invited him to live with her. He'd never fit. How could she not have seen it before? He'd filled up the empty space in her house to the point where she couldn't breathe, and she was always glad when he went home. She'd never left personal possessions at his house, nor had he at hers.

She'd chalked it up to the fact she'd never lived with anyone other than Jess, but now she realized it was just him. She had mentally forced him to fit because she thought it was what she wanted—a partner—and she was afraid time was running out on that prospect. Her impending fortieth birthday had made her life decisions seem urgent.

She left his house for the last time, then sat in her car, contemplating what to do next. She'd learned what she didn't want from a partner, so what did she want? She would have to give it some thought.

What she knew for sure was that with Riley around—and Daniel—she was relaxed.

And she laughed.

Ted was right. It was reason to celebrate—not her freedom from Ted, but her freedom to enjoy her life.

She got out her cell phone from her purse and dialed Daniel's number.

"What's up?" he asked.

"I have a proposition for you."

DANIEL MOVED into her house that night. He would share Riley's room. Without the responsibility of taking care of Riley during the day, he could work on his projects. Three weeks remained until he had to report to the university for the new semester. He could go home now, of course, since Maureen was on vacation, but neither of them brought it up as an option.

"Do you want to talk about it? About Ted?" Daniel asked after Riley went to bed and they'd settled in the living room.

"I'm okay."

"I can see that, but that doesn't mean you don't need to talk it out."

"I feel bad that I hurt him, but I'm so relieved, Daniel. I can't even tell you how much."

"How'd he take it?"

"Like a man." She softened the words. "He was angry and hurt, and controlled both very well. He made sure I knew there were other fish in the sea who've been circling him. That's how I knew for sure I'd done the right thing. It didn't bother me."

"Much."

After a moment she nodded. "There was a little sting, I admit. You can't turn off your feelings that quickly."

"What about work?"

"I'll go into the office tomorrow morning and talk to Bernadette. She'd already planned for me to be gone next week, so it's only this week that matters. I can make some compromises, work from home a little, if necessary. I think she'll be happy that it'll free you up to devote more time to your project. She's been worried, given that we've promised distribution on certain dates for various ShortTakes. It wouldn't look good not to fulfill our obligations so early in the process." She brushed her hands along the arms of the overstuffed chair that she'd reclaimed solely as hers. "I'm sorry if it's taking time away from Sunny."

"I highly doubt that."

She smiled slightly. "I'm taking the Fifth."

"You don't like her."

"She's Anza's friend."

"You don't like her."

"We don't have anything in common."

"You don't like her."

"Okay, okay. I don't like her. She's…blatant."

"I stopped seeing her weeks ago. Or rather, she stopped seeing me."

"Why?"

He grinned. "I'm taking the Fifth."

"You haven't found someone new?"

"I've had a number of dates."

Maureen picked at the fabric beneath her fingers. "Good."

"You didn't expect me to sit around and…wait, did you?"

Wait? For what? "I've always admired your humility, Daniel."

"I like the company of women."

"Yet you've never remarried."

"Once burned, twice shy."

"You never had a desire to have another child?"

"Not since Riley came along. He filled the need. How about you?"

"Not until lately."

"The biological clock is ticking?"

"I'll turn forty on Saturday. Of course it's ticking."

"Would you really like to have another child at this point in your life?"

"It would probably be easier now. Even though I'm older, I'm more financially secure and more patient."

"Do you remember how much energy it takes?"

"I seem to have a lot of energy these days."

"It's the food plan you've been on."

She didn't want to give him the satisfaction of agreeing. She'd even enjoyed the vegetarian dishes he'd prepared, hadn't missed meat at all. Her clothes had gotten a little looser, too, probably because she'd been more active with Riley.

"You won't give me credit for my contribution to your improved health?" he asked. "If you'd exercise just a little more—"

"I don't have time. And you may run, and eat better than I do, but I'm ten years younger. That makes us even."

He laughed and raised his hands in surrender.

"Anyway, it hasn't seemed to stop you from being attracted," she remarked.

"True."

True. A four-letter word with forty-letter impact. "We never talked about that discussion we had a few weeks ago." *About how we have the hots for each other.*

"I had intended to apologize for it that night. Then things got hectic, and I didn't. And then I decided to just let it go. There was nothing either of us could do about it. Did you wonder?"

Time for honesty, she decided. "Yes."

"You could've brought up the subject, too, you know."

"I didn't feel I had the right."

"So. Now what?"

"I don't know. How's this for a segue—I just broke up with Ted *today*," she said, not sure of where things were headed between them.

He moved in front of her chair and rested his hands on her armrests, bringing himself close. She focused on his mouth.

"And for a little while," he said, "you're going to wonder if men find you sexy, if there'll be someone else to take Ted's place, if you made a big mistake by letting him go. Rest easy, Double-D. They'll be there in droves."

"Does Grandma have something wrong with her face?" came their grandson's voice from the dark behind them.

Daniel pushed himself upright.

"No, sweetie," Maureen said, grateful Daniel hadn't been kissing her. Sort of grateful, anyway. "Why?"

"'Cause Papa was looking hard at it."

"I had something in my eye," she said, standing. She came up to him, took his hand and headed back toward the guest room. "It's gone now."

She returned a minute later. "Close call," she said quietly.

Daniel nodded. "I made a little office space for myself in your basement. I'll see you in the morning."

So he was ducking out, done with the conversation. But nothing was resolved, and she would continue to wonder where things stood with them. "Okay."

"Thanks for inviting me. I'd about reached my limit at Ty's. I can't believe I was ever that young and sloppy. 'Night."

CHAPTER 16

Rileyism # 48: "She wiggles too much."

The first thing Maureen saw on her desk the next morning was a note asking her to go to Bernadette's office.

"Close the door. Have a seat." She looked directly at Maureen. "Ted called me last night and said you'd broken up."

"Yes."

"Are you all right?"

What could she say? Ted was Bernadette's friend. Maureen couldn't very well tell her how happy and relieved she was. "I'll be fine."

"He also said you plan to take this week as vacation."

How nice of him to do her talking for her—his way of exacting revenge, she supposed. "My first order of business this morning was to ask. Two weeks, actually. I'd like to keep Riley until Jess comes back, whenever that is."

"And if I say no? That I need you here?"

"Then I would try to strike a compromise, maybe work at home some."

Bernadette leaned back. "Contrary to what you may

believe, Maureen, I do understand your need to be with your grandson. I'm very much aware of how much of my children's and my grandchildren's lives I've been missing since Carlos died."

"We need more staff, so that you don't have to do so much."

"More staff wouldn't help at this point. Until these two projects are on the market and getting good reaction, I'm the one it falls to. I owe Carlos that. You know our story, Maureen. He found me working graveyard shift in a convenience store. I was angry at the world, and he was the gentlest of souls. He changed my whole world, gave me a home, a family, self-esteem. Confidence. Primero was his baby. I can't let it falter. His legacy must be preserved at all costs."

"Even at the cost of your own health and well-being?"

"I can tough it out for a few months longer. I promise I'll reorganize the company and delegate more." She waved a hand, dismissing the subject. "On a similar topic, I want you to know that I offered the vice presidency of operations to Doug. He accepted."

Maureen felt gut punched. She hadn't admitted to herself how much she'd wanted the job until it was taken away. She couldn't even speak.

"I don't think you have the fire anymore, Maureen. I need someone with fire. So, go enjoy your grandson. If we have questions, we'll call, but we'll try not to pester you too much. I know your files are in perfect order, and we should be able to find answers to questions easily."

Maureen stood. She walked to the door.

"Maureen?"

She turned.

"I appreciate how concerned you've been for me. We've been good friends for a long time, and I value how you set aside your role as employee to also be a friend. Everyone else has walked on eggshells around me."

Maureen nodded, made an inane remark and left. She'd hoped that their friendship would help her get the promotion, but in the end, it had probably hurt her. And who knew what part Ted had played, if any? She didn't want to look too closely at the possibility.

All she knew for sure was that she'd given almost twenty years of her life to Primero Publishing, and the happiness quotient in the company had always been such that people rarely left. Doug Fairlane was four years younger than Maureen. Although there were other vice president jobs within the company, chances were that he would stay VP of operations for the rest of his career.

Which left no room for promotion for her. She didn't want to be VP of sales, wasn't qualified to be VP of production. That left her as the author liaison for the next twenty-five years.

Was that what she wanted? To live in the same house and do the same job for the next twenty-five years?

Was Daniel right? Would there be droves of men who would find her attractive? Or just one good one—which was all she really wanted? Someone who would be interested in becoming a father?

Anza slipped into Maureen's office as she ran through her files and made notes for whoever would be handling the authors in her absence. Maureen had called her last night and told her about Ted and about taking her vacation starting now.

"Stop with the look," Maureen said, making herself smile, easy to do with her best friend. "I'm fine."

"Did you hear about, um—"

"Doug? Yes."

"And you're still fine?"

"It hurts a little. No, it hurts a lot. But it's not the end of the world."

"I told Bernadette about the baby." She rested a hand on her slightly rounded belly. "She'd already guessed."

"Yeah, well, Anza, it's busting out all over," Maureen said with a laugh. "Did you ask her about working from home?"

"She's going to think it over."

"And if she won't let you?"

"I don't know. I'm sure there are other jobs where I can telecommute, but I hate to leave Primero." She looked around and lowered her voice. "Although the way things are going in the company, maybe a move wouldn't be so bad."

"Bernadette's going to get it together, Anza. She's got the ability and the motivation. She just needs to delegate more and find balance in her life again."

"You really think so?"

"I'm convinced of it."

"Okay. Well, I've got lots of time until I need to worry about it. So. Two weeks off, hmm?"

"That's the plan."

"And Daniel has moved into your house?"

"That's right."

"And you no longer have a boyfriend. You are a free woman."

Maureen decided not to answer. She didn't know what lay ahead.

"I guess having Riley around," Anza said, "will keep you from getting too carried away."

Maureen raised her brows.

"Not very forthcoming, are you?"

Maureen smiled.

"Okay. Have a great vacation." Anza moved toward the door. "By the way, Sunny said Daniel was the best she'd ever had."

Maureen stared at the empty doorway. Her body tingled at Anza's revelation. She had decisions to make. So did Daniel. They'd acknowledged their mutual attraction, but there was so much more to consider before they acted on it—*if* they acted on it. Like their future relationship as grandparents to the same child—a lifelong connection that put them in proximity for the rest of their lives. If they slept together, that memory would always be there, the big elephant in the tiny room.

And there was Jess to consider. If she found out…

Maureen grabbed her briefcase and headed for home.

She felt good. No, she felt great. She'd never taken off two weeks in a row before. Two weeks. She could take Riley somewhere fun. Daniel had taken him everywhere in the city, but she was sure there were places Riley wouldn't mind going to again.

The bus was almost empty during her ride home. The morning marine layer cast a grayish tint over the city, but it only added to the charm of San Francisco. One of the things she loved most about the city was the weather—cool in the summer, warm in the fall, mild the rest of the year. There was nowhere else on earth she would like to live.

She felt incredibly joyful and light. She couldn't remember feeling this good in…forever.

"I'm home," Maureen called as she stepped through her front door. It was only nine-fifteen. The whole day loomed temptingly.

"Grandma, come quick," Riley shouted from the living room. "The dolphin's having a baby."

Maureen had seen more animal births and deaths in the past six weeks than in her entire lifetime. Riley watched each moment with relish and fascination. He ignored *Sesame Street* altogether—"They're puppets, Grandma. I don't *like* puppets." The only cartoons he liked were ones with characters who had superhuman skills and talents.

He was such a stereotypical boy. He loved dirt, bugs, peanut butter and warfare. He could be bloodthirsty, always willing to play swordfight or shootout, and then he would flash that million-watt smile that was innocence personified. She looked forward to seeing him grow up, to seeing who he became as a man.

She had to admit the dolphin birth was fascinating, not icky at all, unlike some of the others she'd been witness to, the kangaroo being by far the strangest.

"Everything go okay at the office?" Daniel asked when a commercial came on.

"Bernadette giveth and Bernadette taketh away." She sat on the opposite end from him on the sofa. "Vacation approved. Promotion denied."

He gave her a look of sympathy. "Her loss."

"Thanks."

"Did she say why?"

"She thinks I no longer have the fire."

"Meaning, the devotion to job and company?"

Maureen nodded.

"Do you agree with her?"

"No. Although I can see how she might feel that way, given what's been happening recently. Ted also took it upon himself to call her last night and tell her I'd ended things with him. They're friends, you know."

"You think that had some impact on her decision?"

"I hope not." But she was coming to believe there was much more to Ted than met the eye. He knew how to manipulate. She would never know if he'd manipulated her.

Daniel angled closer and set a hand on her shoulder. "Can I get you some tea?"

"It's too early for a margarita, I guess." She smiled at him.

"It's five o'clock somewhere."

She waved a dismissive hand. "Just kidding. Tea would be great. Plain green tea, though. Not that herbal/organic/tastes-like-swill stuff you like, okay?"

He just laughed at her.

Riley climbed into her lap. She wrapped her arms around him, his warm little body relaxed and comforting. "Did you have breakfast?" she asked.

"I did. Kashi and bananas. It was good. Did you have breakfast, Grandma?"

"I had the same thing." It was all she could find in the kitchen. She'd pretty much turned over the running of the house to Daniel, a shift so gradual she'd barely noticed, until she realized she hadn't been to the grocery story in weeks. There was always food in the refrigerator, always something delicious left over to heat up. He'd totally spoiled her.

Daniel returned with two mugs of tea. She eyed him as he set hers on the end table, then sat down and sipped from his own.

Sunny said Daniel was the best she'd ever had.

Anza's exit line stuck with Maureen, a whisper in her ear, a hazy dream in her imagination. What made him different? What made him the best?

"Do I have dirt on my face?" the man in question asked, his mug an inch from his mouth.

She couldn't feed his ego by telling him the truth, although plenty of women had probably told him already. He'd more than hinted before that he was a good lover, but she'd come to realize through the years that everyone considered themselves a good lover.

His status as such had been confirmed by Sunny, who had enough experience to know the difference.

"You okay?" Daniel asked.

She snapped into focus. "What happened between you and Sunny?"

He raised his brows, his glance dipping to Riley. She clamped her mouth shut.

"I don't like Sunny," Riley said, not looking away from the television.

"You only met her once," Daniel said. "At the Fourth of July picnic."

"She wiggles too much."

Maureen smiled over Riley's head at Daniel. "Well, Mr. Riley, what would you like to do on Grandma's first day of vacation?"

"I wanna take the dinners to the old people with Auntie Cherie."

"She doesn't do the Mobile Meals on Monday. We can call her and ask if we could go tomorrow."

"Can we go see Mr. K.? Remember, Papa, how much he liked it when we pushed his wheelchair up the hill?"

"I remember."

"We should do that again."

"Okay."

He shifted on her lap until he could look at her. "When my mommy and I go home, I'm gonna see if we can take dinners to people. I think my mommy would make people smile, too, like Auntie Cherie."

"Like *you*. That's very kind of you, Riley."

He shrugged.

"At three o'clock there's craft hour at the library," Daniel said. "We made papier-mâché masks last week. Today the kids are supposed to paint them."

"You want to do that, Riley?"

"Yeah!"

"Would you like to go to the park this morning while Papa works?"

"Okay. Can we bring Morgan?"

"Remember, her daddy's here on leave, so she probably wants to be with him."

"I forgot."

Maureen had a surprise for him. "And…you and I are going to Discovery Kingdom. They've got dolphins and whales, and lions and tigers."

"Today?"

"In two days."

"Aw, Grandma."

"Well, today we're going to the library to paint your mask. And tomorrow with Auntie Cherie to deliver food. Should we skip doing those things, too?"

"I wanna do *everything*."

"Me, too." She stood, setting him on his feet. "So, let's turn off the television and head to the park. We need to let Papa work. Go get your sneakers and a sweatshirt, please."

He took off running.

"You seem happy," Daniel commented, scrutinizing her.

"I am."

"Why?" he asked, standing and moving closer.

She ticked off the items on her fingers as she spoke. "Jess forgave me for not being the world's greatest mother. I forgave her for not being the world's greatest daughter. I forgave my father for not being the world's greatest father. He forgave me for not being the world's greatest daughter."

"That's all?" He grinned.

"Yeah. Just minor stuff."

"When did all this happen?"

"In the past few days. Then I broke up with Ted, which was like forgiving myself for not being the world's greatest girlfriend."

"Self-forgiveness is important to good mental health."

"So I've discovered." She cupped his arm for a moment. "What happened between you and Sunny?"

"She was getting too serious."

"But you said she broke it off with you, not the other way around."

"She backed me into a corner and wanted answers, then she didn't like my answers, so she ended it."

"What kind of answers?"

"No, I wasn't interested in anything long-term. No, I wasn't interested in moving here. No, I wasn't interested in having her move to Seattle. No, I'm not interested in marriage—ever."

His posture had gone more rigid with each sentence. Maureen backed off just as Riley charged back into the room, his sweatshirt on backward, his shoes on but not tied. *I'm not interested in marriage—ever.*

"And in case you're wondering, Maureen—and I think you are—I've been too busy working on the ShortTakes to concentrate on anyone else."

"I wasn't wondering."

He half smiled, challenging her.

"Maybe I was wondering a little bit," she said, tying Riley's shoes.

"I've been curious about you and you-know-who, too, and why you ended it."

"As you noted, he had turned into boyfriend-in-title-only. But we'll talk later, you and I. Okay, buddy boy, let's go."

"Bye, Papa."

"Have fun."

The day was beyond fun. Maureen's relationship with Riley was so comfortable now that she could barely remember when it wasn't. They played at the park until they were pleasantly tired, then stopped by the PeaceLove Café and picked up a pesto pizza for lunch so that Daniel wouldn't have to cook—or, rather, she wouldn't. She had to stop thinking in terms of him doing everything. She was on vacation, and he was working.

After lunch Daniel returned to the basement to work, Riley lay down for a rest, and Maureen stretched out on a chaise lounge in the backyard with a novel but soon set her book aside and closed her eyes. The sun broke through and bathed her with warmth. Healing warmth.

Healing? There was no other word for it. She felt healthy and strong in ways that astonished her, because she hadn't been aware of feeling unhealthy or weak before—not until today, when she felt the opposite. Today she knew what she'd been missing.

After Riley's nap it was time to go to the library. She hollered down the stairs to Daniel that they were leaving.

"We both made masks," he called up. "Feel free to paint mine to suit yourself."

In the library's craft room, nine children crowded around a short, round, washable table, sharing mayonnaise jars of paint and chunky paintbrushes as their parents/siblings/ babysitters offered help and tried to paint their own masks while holding them in the air. Maureen splattered red paint on her jeans; Riley dripped dots of yellow and blue, turning her into a live primary-color display.

When they were done painting, they left the masks on the table to dry, then sat on the floor to listen to the children's librarian do a dramatic reading of *Stone Soup*, followed by a lively puppet show presentation of *Three Billy Goats Gruff*. After juice and cookies, everyone held their masks over their faces while the librarian read *How to Care for Your Monster*, a book about funny monsters, everyone joining in the fun.

As they played, Riley giggled and screeched. He called Maureen Grandma Monster, which shortly became Gramster.

As they walked home, he held up his mask at anyone they met on the street, drawing smiles from passersby. The only time he stepped out of character was when a super-stretch Hummer limo went by. Fascinated, he stared open-mouthed. "Look how long it is," he said in awe.

"As long as a city bus." She was no less awed.

"I wanna ride in it."

"Me, too. I've never been in a limo."

"Me, neither. Do you think they have a television in it?"

"One that gets *Animal Planet?*" she asked, grinning.

He grinned back. "Yeah."

"I'm sure they do. And a refrigerator and a bar. And I've heard that some of them have a hot tub."

He frowned. "Who'd want to take a bath in a limo? I'd want to stand up and look at everything through that window on top, wouldn't you?"

How could she answer that? *It depends, Riley, whether I'm riding with you or your sexy grandpa.*

"You know what else would be fun?" she asked, changing the subject.

"What?"

"A trip to Hawaii."

"Yeah." He paused. "What's a Hawaii?"

"Paradise."

"Have you been there?"

"Not yet. Someday." She lifted her mask into place. "I'll race you home."

He beat her even without her intentionally throwing the

race. Once inside he ran down the hallway, heading toward the basement to scare Daniel, but Daniel was in the kitchen cooking something—*another* something—deliciously aromatic.

Riley veered toward the kitchen. "Look, Papa! Look what Gramster and I made."

Daniel admired Riley's wildly painted mask then looked at Maureen, who had put her mask over her face and growled and prowled toward Riley, who screamed and hid behind Daniel, laughing ecstatically.

"Gramster?" Daniel queried.

"Grandma plus monster equals…"

"Ah." He grinned as Riley peeked out. "I take it you had fun, bud."

"Hecka fun, Papa. It was awesome."

"Why are you cooking?" she asked. "You're working. I'm on vacation. My turn to take over the cooking again."

"I'd done as much as I could for one day. Cooking relaxes me."

"Are you serious?"

"Yeah, why?"

"I must be doing something wrong. Cooking makes me tense. Got to get everything done at the same time and all that."

"You worry too much."

"I suppose I do. Riley, you need to wash your face and hands."

"Can I watch *Animal Planet?*"

She decided he needed some downtime. "For a little while."

"Looks like Gramster had fun, too," Daniel commented after Riley left.

"Hecka fun. He's going to sleep well tonight."

Daniel stirred the pot. "And after he's asleep, we'll have that talk you mentioned."

I'm not interested in marriage—ever. The words that had whispered in her head all day sounded louder suddenly. Did she really want to get closer—to reveal her secret hurts—to a man who would be in her life forever, but not intimately?

She walked away without answering him, allowing herself the few hours until Riley went to bed to make up her mind.

THE HOUSE WAS extraordinarily quiet with Riley asleep and the television off. Maureen put on a Diana Krall CD, lowered the volume, then sat in her chair, tucking her legs under her. Daniel brought two glasses of white zinfandel. He passed her one then took a seat on the sofa.

"Looks like 'Gramster' is going to stick with Riley," he said.

"I hope so. It's fun." She'd gotten what she wished for, after all—that special name. And if she hadn't taken time off from work and kept him while Jess was gone with Keith, it wouldn't have happened. Maureen had no regrets for how everything had turned out.

She sipped her wine, then toasted Daniel. "Very nice."

"I'm glad to see the merlot gone. Not my favorite," Daniel said, lifting his glass, as well, before he drank from it.

Was there a double meaning behind his words? Substitute *Ted* for *merlot*?

"So," he said.

"So."

"All the forgiveness you've been giving and receiving— I take it it's been overdue."

She nodded.

"So, why now?"

"Timing and opportunity. And a need to make changes in my life. It was most important that I forgive my father, because that led to forgiving myself both as a daughter and a mother."

"What about Jess's father?" Daniel leaned forward. "Why doesn't she talk about him?"

"Because he never acknowledged her."

"Who was he?"

"He owned the company where I got my first job shortly after my seventeenth birthday. I was a part-time file clerk and receptionist. He was in his thirties."

"Married?"

"Separated—or so he said. I found out too late he wasn't honest about anything. But he was older and experienced, and he saw that I hadn't found a place in the world and was ripe for someone to flatter me and pay attention to me. And guide me."

"He neglected to take charge of birth control, or even to teach you about it?"

"I knew the basics, but I was so blinded by infatuation that I didn't do anything about it."

"*He* should have."

"Yes. But then, I got Jess out of the deal, so I don't resent that, just the way he treated me. As if I were a liar. As if I'd gone after *him*."

"I suppose you know about statutory rape."

"More than I ever thought I'd need to know."

"Since you obviously didn't get married, did he end up in jail?"

"I didn't name him. Everyone tried to make me, but I never said who the father was."

"Not even for the birth certificate?"

She shook her head. "Especially not."

"Why?"

"Because he would've been arrested. And I was scared. He made me feel like I was the guilty one."

"He should've been arrested. And locked away."

"You're absolutely right, but it wouldn't have helped my situation."

"Maybe it would've stopped him from preying on others who followed you. That's a pattern a man like that doesn't break, Maureen."

"At seventeen I didn't know that."

"What happened after you found out you were pregnant?"

She was squeezing her wineglass so hard that she had to set it aside. "He offered to pay for an abortion. I refused. I went to Cherie for help. She made me tell my father. When I wouldn't name the father, he kicked me out. Cherie took me in. Jess's father got scared that I was going to complicate his life, so he offered me a lot of money—cash, of course—if I would never contact him again, never tell my child who her father was, and would sign a document denying he was the father."

Daniel frowned but said nothing.

"I almost turned down the money. I was a teenager—what did I know? I wanted to prove I could do it myself, that I didn't need him or his money for anything. But Cherie gave me an entirely different perspective. She convinced me to take what he offered, then helped me find investments to make it grow, so that when Jess was six and I'd been working for a few years, I could afford to buy us a house."

"And this guy has never contacted you or looked for his daughter?"

"No. And me, always the peacekeeper, I've made sure that we could be easily found."

He pushed himself off the couch then didn't go anywhere. "I think a lot of men get off the hook because girls won't point the finger. Maybe because I'm a teacher I see it more often—what unplanned pregnancy can do to a young woman."

Maureen studied him as he swigged the rest of his wine. "You know, Daniel, I've come to realize that Jess really did need you these past years. You are to Jess what Cherie has been to me. I hadn't seen the similarity until now. Jess didn't need just a father figure, but you in particular. I always thought you were far too liberal and a little, well, strange. I was really off the mark."

"I know I was indulgent, but I think she turned out okay."

He should've gotten married. Should've been a father again. "So did Riley. It's fun to watch the two of you together."

After a moment he smiled. "Well, would you look at us? We're not only getting along, we're complimenting each other."

"With any luck, it'll stay that way."

"Oh, I don't know. I miss the sparring. It always revs me up."

"Given what I know of you, you're in a perpetual state of rev."

He was quiet for a while. "I admit I date a lot. Maybe too much. Perhaps my fatal flaw is that I focus on what's wrong with a woman rather than what's right, so it's easy to let them go."

"Or push them away?"

"Maybe."

"Is that how you're going to live the rest of your life—flitting from woman to woman, never having a partner?"

"Have you checked out the divorce rate?" He set his glass aside and moved to stand in front of the picture window, his hands stuffed in his pockets. He vibrated with tension, and probably with unspoken words.

"I'm going out," he said after a moment. "See you in the morning."

Maureen didn't react to his sudden departure, didn't say good-night. Unburdening herself was supposed to make her feel better, and for a little while she had felt…unburdened, especially since he'd been nonjudgmental. But not now. Now they were back to square one—defensive. She didn't even know why.

Maureen watched television until late, then went to bed after she caught herself falling asleep sitting up. But in bed she stayed awake, waiting for Daniel to come home, wondering where he was. Finally she heard him return. He stopped by her door. She held her breath, waiting, then he walked away.

She didn't know whether to be disappointed or grateful. She hoped he was being careful of her feelings since she'd just broken up with Ted, but then the same pattern continued night after night. He would go out after dinner or down to the basement office, and she wouldn't see him until the next morning.

Several days passed like that. She had finally resigned herself to just being happy that they were getting along, to the fact that the status quo had to be good enough, when their relationship suddenly changed.

The night started differently. Daniel hung around after dinner instead of going out or to the basement. He played with Riley and eyed Maureen in an unusual way. Tension between them had built day by day. The progress they'd been making in their relationship had come to a screeching halt the night he'd moved in. She didn't understand why he'd been acting that way, but the result was he was making it much easier for her to see him leave when Jess returned for Riley.

She'd been a fool to think there might be more. She'd confided in him about how she'd let herself get pregnant, and he'd been angry that she hadn't prosecuted Kirk. Daniel had apparently lost any respect he had for her. Or maybe now that she wouldn't be quite as much of a challenge, he'd lost interest. He probably felt stuck at her place until Jess came back.

After Riley went to bed, Daniel stayed on the couch watching television, but nothing else happened. Just a slight change in routine, she decided, and uttered a quick goodnight, then went to bed.

He couldn't go back to Seattle fast enough, Maureen thought, punching her pillow later after yet another sleepless night, even though this time he was at home.

She didn't even relax when she finally heard him walk past her bedroom toward the guest room. She wanted to jump out of bed and tell him what she thought of him, that the tension he was creating was getting to her.

She *almost* regretted giving up Ted, who at least never kept her wondering....

Well, no. She wouldn't go that far.

She closed her eyes and tried to drift to sleep, then came a knock on her bedroom door just before it swung open.

Daniel leaned into the room.

"What's wrong?" she asked, startled.

He came in without an invitation. Light from the living room behind him cast him in silhouette as he moved toward the bed. She sat up. Had he gotten drunk since she'd gone to bed?

He sat beside her, facing her, his silence sending waves of curiosity through her. As he remained silent, anxiety crept in. Then he put a hand around the back of her neck and pulled her toward him. His lips settled on hers, boldly, confidently.

He didn't taste of alcohol but of desire, barely restrained. She didn't have to wonder anymore—he kissed like a dream. Her body seemed to fill with lava, heavy and hot. She wrapped her arms around him and moved closer. He changed angles, deepening the kiss. This was a man who knew what he was doing and did it well. She finally got to touch his hair, his thick, tempting hair. She threaded her fingers through it then grabbed hold. *Touch me, touch me, touch me....*

But he didn't. He eased away from her and left the room, still without speaking, leaving her aroused and agitated... and totally baffled.

CHAPTER 17

Rileyism #49: "I don't want the boat to get wet."

The next day Maureen embraced her fortieth birthday as a milestone instead of a millstone. Daniel and Riley had huddled frequently during the week, after which Riley would grin secretively at Maureen. Sometimes he would say, "Guess what, Gramster?" and Daniel would shush him. She figured they were plotting a surprise for her birthday.

Well, she had a few surprises up her sleeve, as well. She left home early on Saturday morning, the day of her birthday, to keep her appointment for a self-indulgent spa day. She treated herself to a massage, facial, manicure and pedicure, then she gave in to her stylist's long-begged-for wish and let him cut and color her hair, deepening the red to a richer color and cutting it a few inches into a straight, sassy, contemporary style.

She had her makeup done, a new look for the first time in at least ten years. A stranger looked back from the mirror, but it was a stranger she liked.

Next, new clothes, from the inside out. Sexy, lacy

lingerie like nothing she'd owned before, and several new outfits to wear away from the office. Man grabbers, the sales clerk called them, trendy and flattering. The Rowdies would be proud of her.

She left the store wearing a formfitting, forest-green knit V-neck top with matching pants and high-heeled sandals. She even sprang for a new necklace and earrings, gold with green stones.

Daniel's kiss from last night haunted her. What did it mean? Why didn't he say anything? What would happen now? What did she *want* to happen now?

She had no answers. Well, maybe she had a few answers. And needs. And desires.

Maureen met up with Cherie late in the afternoon in the lobby lounge of the Ritz-Carlton for afternoon tea, a birthday tradition since Maureen's fifteenth birthday when they'd moved to the Bay Area. The special birthday celebration was a life event she counted on. The lounge's crystal chandeliers and old portraits were soothing in their familiarity, as was the harp music and the view of the city skyline and the garden courtyard.

Cherie was standing near the hostess's podium as Maureen approached. Her aunt eyed her briefly, then looked away, not recognizing Maureen. Then Cherie suddenly made eye contact as she realized it was her niece.

Cherie's smile was quick and wide. "You look stunning, my dear. Absolutely stunning."

"I *feel* good."

They followed the hostess to their chairs and settled in. Cherie continued to smile. "So, what prompted all this?"

"Turning forty," Maureen answered.

"Not a certain sexy grandpa?"

Maureen shrugged. "He might have had a little to do with it. He likes to point out when I'm being stodgy, as he terms it." He'd even caught her ironing her jeans the other day and pulled the plug on the iron while shaking his head. "He's been a daily reminder not to let myself get old before my time. So has Riley."

"Have Daniel and Riley seen your update?"

"You're the first."

Their server approached, and they ordered the traditional tea selection from the menu, as always, one that came with a variety of finger sandwiches, scones and tea cakes. They ordered pots of the two teas they always ordered—China Rose Petal and Snow Dragon.

Maureen reached across and laid her hand on her aunt's. "Thank you so much for this wonderful tradition. I love it. And I love you so much."

Cherie's eyes went bright. "I love you, too, dear. Very, very much. And I thank you for making peace with your father. It means a lot to him."

"To me, too."

They savored their light meal, especially the scones with Devonshire cream, lemon curd and strawberry preserves, their favorite of all the offerings, then lingered with tea and conversation.

"No regrets about giving up Ted?" Cherie asked as they each sipped their last cup.

"None. You were right about him. He needed everything done his way. No compromising." Maureen emptied her cup and set it down. "I'd like to ask you a really personal question, which you don't have to feel obligated to answer."

"I think I can guess. You want to know why I've never married, right?"

Maureen nodded.

"I'm surprised you waited all these years to ask. You know, it wasn't really a choice I made, but something that simply evolved through time. At first there was college, then my hippie days, which I wouldn't trade for anything. After that, you and your father to take care of, twice. Then you came to live with me when you were pregnant, and you and Jess both needed me. Please don't misunderstand me—I was glad to do it and haven't regretted it for a moment…."

She shook her head slowly. "No. It's time to tell the truth, especially to myself. I don't regret the time I gave to your father and you, but I do regret not marrying and having children. I did date, quite a bit actually." She looked at Maureen over the rim of her cup. "I was proposed to three times."

"You didn't love any of them?"

"One, I did. Just one. He was a beautiful man, inside and out."

"So why did you turn him down?"

"I didn't think I was good enough for him."

"Cherie! You're the best person I know. How could you think that?"

"We all have misperceptions about ourselves, don't we? Years later I kept seeing myself in you, kept trying to urge you to live your life differently than I did, more fully, but you were even more dutiful and responsible than I was."

"Because I learned my lesson the hard way by getting pregnant because I was rebelling against all the rules Dad put on me."

"I know. I did try to balance him out on the grand scale of life."

Maureen smiled. "I know. You *did,* too. My only regret is not having another child."

"But, dear, you're not too old to have another child."

"Finding a man at this age who's interested in that particular commitment isn't easy, Cherie. And then there's the whole finding-the-man factor itself."

Not to mention getting Daniel out of her system first, with or without sleeping with him.

"Just be careful when it comes to Daniel," Cherie cautioned, as if reading Maureen's mind.

"Meaning?"

"He's a heartbreaker, isn't he?"

Daniel's words about not being interested in marriage—ever—already echoed in her head several times a day.

Slightly subdued by their conversation, Maureen drove Cherie home, then stayed a while because Daniel had told her not to come home until six o'clock. At promptly six o'clock she unlocked her front door and stepped inside to a quiet house. No sounds of a boy vrooming cars. No sounds of a lioness hunting down prey to feed her king of the jungle. Post-death-knell quiet.

She set her packages aside then almost tiptoed down the hall, wondering if people would jump out and yell surprise. She stopped just before the doorway to the living room and peeked around the corner.

"Happy Birthday, Gramster!"

Riley stood at attention next to Daniel. They both held bouquets of red roses and wore tuxedos.

"Oh, my goodness! Look at you." Maureen didn't want to ruin her makeup, but she couldn't stop her tears at seeing the sweetest little boy in the world all dressed up—for her. Not to mention the dashing, sexy man beside him. The elusive man…

Riley walked carefully toward her and presented her with his bouquet, then he bowed before breaking into giggles and hugging her. "You look pretty," he said.

"Thank you. The flowers are beautiful, sweetie."

Daniel came up behind Riley and passed her the rest of the bouquet. "You look hot," he mouthed, then he leaned across and kissed her cheek, not an innocent peck between friends, but the sexiest, most seductive kiss on the cheek ever, his warm breath dusting her ear, giving her the shivers, confusing her more than ever.

"Have you had a good day?" he asked, moving back, his expression intense.

"I had a great day."

"You look amazing. You looked great before, but this is…wow."

Riley yanked on her top. "Guess what? Guess what? We're going—"

Daniel clamped his hands on Riley's shoulders. "Not yet. Surprises, remember?"

Riley looked up at his grandfather, a twinkle in his eyes, nearly bursting with keeping whatever the surprise was to himself. He grinned then covered his mouth.

"Good job." Daniel glanced at his watch then Maureen. "You have time to put your flowers in a vase and grab a coat."

"I'm not dressed up enough. You're in tuxes."

"You're dressed fine. Really."

"But I bought something…." Oh, yeah, she'd bought something, all right. Something slinky, with a deep V neckline, in a dark purple that flattered her hair and complexion.

"Then by all means change," he said, reaching for the roses. "I'll put these in water."

When she returned to the living room twenty minutes later, she was nervous and excited. She knew the dress flattered her. Daniel didn't have to tell her she looked good to him—he showed her with the sharpening of his gaze, the flexing of his jaw, the rigidity of his posture.

They walked to the front door together, Riley leading the way.

"Is that a bit of lace I spy, Double-D?" Daniel whispered, his gaze focused on her chest. "Did you take my advice?"

She decided it wasn't the time to be coy. "Yes and yes."

"It's extremely cruel of you to tease, you know."

"Payback is hell," she said.

"Payback for what?"

"The irritating nickname. The years of general antagonism." *The occasional bold, flattering look you gave me. The way you kept me confused all week, especially last night. The kiss. The wonderful kiss.*

He flashed a grin. "If this is your idea of payback, I think I'll keep antagonizing you."

"It's here, Papa! It's here!"

Maureen glanced in the direction Riley was pointing. A black limousine was double-parked in front of the house. She looked in astonishment at Daniel.

"A little bird mentioned that you'd never ridden in one before," he said. "Sorry it's not a Hummer."

"You've outdone yourself," she said to Daniel as Riley hopped down the stairs. "Don't go into the street," she called out to him as the driver got out of the car and walked around to open the door for them.

"I won't," Riley said, all the while bouncing and hopping, waiting for them to catch up, looking like an impatient penguin in his tux.

Maureen grabbed his hand, smiled at the driver, then climbed inside.

"Happy birthday, Mom!"

Maureen almost fell face forward as she looked up suddenly, hearing Jess's voice.

"You really didn't think we'd miss such a momentous occasion, did you?" Jess asked, hugging her.

"You look beautiful," Maureen said, tears welling up again as she eyed her daughter. She couldn't remember the last time she'd seen Jess wearing a dress, having been a ripped-jeans-and-T-shirt girl forever. But tonight she wore a short, sexy, moss-green crushed-velvet dress. She'd had her golden hair trimmed to just below her shoulders, and it looked soft again, not the *True Grit* dry-and-damaged shape it had been in just a week ago. And she looked happy, like-never-before happy.

Maureen hugged Keith, also looking dapper in a tux, who sat grinning at everyone. Riley climbed into the seat next to Jess as the limo pulled into traffic.

"When did you get here?" Maureen asked her daughter.

"Around noon. Got to spend all afternoon with my sweet boy."

"Where did you spend your week?"

"In the Lake Tahoe area." She gave Riley a big hug. "But I missed this guy too much, so we came to get him so we could all go to Disneyland together."

So. Everything had gone well for Jess and Keith.

"We're going to Disneyland?" Riley asked, his eyes wide.

"We sure are."

"Awesome!" He pumped his fist in the air.

The limo driver took them on a tour of the city that

seemed magical to Maureen even though she'd lived there for so long. Riley acted as tour guide, pointing out all the sights, an expert now about San Francisco.

Tomorrow he would be gone. Maureen swallowed around the lump that formed in her throat. She'd had the time of her life with him, had never gotten so many hugs before, or been snuggled up against so tightly. That adorable grin had flashed a hundred times a day, sometimes in giddiness, sometimes in appreciation, and even sometimes in an attempt—often successful—to con her into something.

Her gaze drifted to her daughter, who looked stunningly beautiful and content. Jess made eye contact then and seemed to see the raw emotions brimming in Maureen, because Jess's smile softened and her gaze gentled. She grabbed her mother's hand. "Everything's good, Mom."

Maureen nodded. She looked away, connecting with Daniel's watchful eyes then. She couldn't read his expression, as he neither smiled nor frowned.

Conversation never lagged during the drive, which ended at one of the piers on the wharf, a large yacht docked alongside it.

"You get to watch the sunset, Gramster! And eat dinner at the same time. Isn't that cool? And Papa says we can dance up a storm, but I don't want to make a storm come. I don't want the boat to get wet."

A dinner-dance sunset cruise around the Bay? "How long have you been plotting this?" she asked Daniel as they walked the pier, Riley holding hands with Jess and Keith ahead of them.

"Since Sunday night."

The day Jess and Keith had left. The day she'd broken up with Ted. The day she'd asked Daniel to move in. "When did you find out Jess would be home?"

"She told me before she and Keith left. I was supposed to tell Ted, in case he planned something. Of course at that point, Jess didn't know you would be breaking up with him. She didn't seem too surprised today when I told her, however."

"She probably figured the handwriting was on the wall when I canceled my vacation with him a second time to keep Riley." She stumbled slightly on the uneven dock. Daniel steadied her, then pulled her arm through his, grazing her breast. She pulled herself closer.

He met her gaze, his eyes darkening.

The moment of anticipation set the tone for the evening, which was the best in Maureen's memory. They consumed an incredible meal as the yacht cruised slowly around San Francisco Bay. While indulging in tiger prawns and roasted Anaheim peppers stuffed with spinach, corn and cheese with saffron rice, they watched the city landmarks and skyline silhouetted and highlighted by the ever-changing angle of the setting sun. A small combo provided music to dine by, then music to dance by. Riley, unencumbered by shyness, danced almost every dance.

The long, busy night caught up with him after he'd eaten

a huge chocolate mousse for dessert, and he stretched out on a cushion and fell asleep. Jess and Keith headed outside to look at the view from on deck. Maureen and Daniel kept the sleeping Riley in sight as they took to the dance floor.

"Alone at last," Daniel said.

She smiled. "If you don't count the other fifty guests."

"They don't count since they aren't staring at us as if we're lab experiments."

Maureen laughed. "Jess isn't subtle at all, is she?"

"No, she's damned curious, and I expect she'll bombard you with questions the minute she can get you alone."

"I expect you're right."

"What will you tell her?"

She picked a piece of lint off his shoulder and flicked it aside. "That we were able to put aside our past differences and be a united front for Riley."

"That all? Anyone can see what's going on between us." He tightened his arm around her waist, bringing her even closer.

Her breath caught at the feel of his body. "What *is* going on?" she managed to ask.

He pulled her impossibly closer.

"Well. At least I can *feel* what's going on between us, even if you won't say," she said, flattered by the proof of his attraction pressed against her abdomen. She laid her head against his shoulder. "Why did you kiss me last night? All week you've been distant. Sometimes I thought you were angry at me, yet last night you came into my bedroom and kissed me."

"I wasn't angry. I had been trying to be sensitive to your just having broken up with Ted."

"Since when are you Mr. Considerate?" She hoped he heard the smile in her voice.

"Believe it or not, most people don't find me inconsiderate at all. It's just been your perception of me." He blew out a breath. "Honestly, though? Mostly, I was just frustrated all week. I didn't dare be alone with you."

He held himself more stiffly.

She leaned back and made eye contact. "I was joking, Daniel. I've learned how considerate and kind you can be."

He stared back for several long seconds. "Sometimes it's hard to separate the past from the present with you."

"You don't trust the newer, better relationship we have?"

"Maybe not completely."

That put a different spin on everything. She'd thought—erroneously, apparently—that they'd found common ground, at least beyond just the physical. "Are you afraid of it?" she asked hesitantly. "Or don't you believe it?"

"It's the riskiest relationship I've had."

"Because of Riley and Jess?"

"Yeah."

She nodded. "I've been debating it, too."

"Did you reach a conclusion?"

The discussion was too businesslike. She wanted to be courted and seduced, not come to logical conclusions. "I think if we talk about it too much, we could talk ourselves out of it."

The song ended, an up-tempo one replacing it. They returned to their seats, a new tension between them. Not long after, the yacht docked.

Maureen glanced at Daniel as Keith carried a sleeping Riley to the limo, catching a bittersweet expression on Daniel's face. Being replaced took some adjusting.

At home, it was decided that Riley would sleep with Maureen, and Jess and Keith would take the guest room, leaving Daniel with the couch. After an hour of tossing and turning, Maureen eased out of bed and left the room. She tiptoed into the kitchen and poured herself a glass of water. A siren blared in the distance, getting closer and closer, then stopping nearby.

She snuck into the living room to look out the window, seeing a fire engine a few houses away. After a moment an ambulance pulled up as well.

She didn't know the people who lived in that house.

"What's going on?" Daniel asked, coming up beside her, his fingertips grazing her back.

She tried not to lean into the touch. "I don't know. Looks like a medical emergency, since I don't see the firemen pulling hose or anything."

"That's Kathy and Dave Emerson's house. They have a brand-new baby, Abby."

Maureen didn't know that. She knew someone had moved in about a month ago, but she hadn't taken cookies to welcome them, something she always did.

"I'm going to see what's happening." He grabbed his

jeans from the coffee table and slipped them on over his briefs, which she'd tried her best to ignore, then pulled on a sweatshirt.

Through the window she saw him hurry barefoot down the front steps. His hands shoved in his pockets, he stopped to talk to a firefighter. It was another facet of him she hadn't known about until recently—he liked people, stopped to talk to them, got to know neighbors, even ones that weren't his.

Somehow it made her failings seem so much bigger.

She should've known who the Emersons were and that they had a new baby.

She'd been preoccupied with work and Riley, and her chance to build a relationship with him, but she'd gotten even more than she'd hoped for. She'd not only made peace with Daniel but had learned from him about how to live more fully, more in the moment. Look at how he'd adapted to Riley being in San Francisco. He'd just gone out, found himself a room and settled in. She not only liked Daniel, she admired him.

A minute later he jogged up the stairs. "Kathy's mother. She's here from Arizona helping with the baby. She was having chest pains that have subsided for now. They're taking her to the hospital." He shivered and rubbed his arms. "I asked if there was some way we could help. They'll let us know."

Maureen put her arms around him, offering warmth. After a minute he did the same, pulling her even closer. His cheek against hers was cool.

"You're a good person," she said.

"Not always."

"I didn't say you were a saint."

He laughed low, the sound vibrating through her body.

"I've tried to be a role model for Riley," he said, his hands moving over her back, massaging, until she almost melted against him. "Looks like Keith is going to assume that job now."

"I hope they don't make decisions too quickly. One week isn't long enough to know someone," she said, completely relaxed, her eyes closed. "Are you dying to know how she did on *True Grit?*"

"I'm curious. I figure she must've gotten pretty far, because she came home looking like she'd been stretched to the limit. If she'd been voted out early, she would've had time to recover before she got here."

"I never thought about it like that." She leaned back, making eye contact. "You don't suppose she won the million dollars?"

"No reason why she couldn't. She was in great shape, she was determined, and she's good at making alliances. Three necessary qualities to win."

Maureen flattened her hands on his chest. "What if she did? What if Keith is after her for her money? I mean, he was on staff, so he knows who won."

"We can suggest a prenup."

Maureen breathed again. "Oh. Oh, of course. Unless they don't get married, and he convinces her to spend all her money on him somehow."

"How?"

She stepped away, needing to think. "I don't know. Get her to buy him a car or a boat or a house. Something like that."

"In his name? Give her credit for having more sense than that."

"Yes, do give me credit."

Maureen and Daniel turned as Jess padded into the room.

"How long have you been there?" Maureen asked.

"Long enough to hear you're worried about Keith being a gold digger. Long enough to see there's something going on between you two."

"Could he be?" Maureen asked, ignoring the second sentence.

"No."

"How do you know that?"

"I just do. You'll have to take my word for it."

"Are you going by instinct, Jess, or do you have proof?"

"Why do you always need proof? Why can't you just trust your gut now and then?"

"I know it's a character flaw." Maureen folded her arms. The truth hurt.

Jess gestured toward Daniel. "And what's going on between you two? You looked like a couple tonight, plus just now…"

"We aren't sleeping together, if that's what you're implying," Maureen said.

"You broke up with Ted."

"That had nothing to do with Daniel." Which wasn't

exactly the truth. Maybe Daniel had helped to open her eyes to the mistake she would've been making had she let that relationship continue. She hoped she would've recognized it herself before it was too late.

"Didn't look like it—"

"That's enough, Jess," Daniel interrupted quietly but firmly.

"You know he loves 'em then leaves 'em," Jess said to Maureen. "I'm sorry, Daniel, but it's true. I don't want to see my mom hurt."

"Your mother knows all there is to know about me. Now, I think it's time to end this discussion."

Jess turned around, making a huffing sound.

"Wait," Maureen said. She caught up with her daughter and took her into her arms. They'd come so far. She didn't want to lose the new, wonderful relationship they'd created. "Thank you for looking out for me," she said to Jess.

Jess hugged her back, hard. "Thank you, too, Mom. I know you mean well."

"Always."

"Keith is good to me and good for me. He loves me. He understands me. I can't tell you about who won, but I can say that Keith and I fell in love before the end of the show. This is the real deal."

"I guess I can't ask for more than that."

Jess kissed Maureen's cheek. "Thank you."

Maureen waited until Jess shut the bedroom door behind her, then turned to Daniel. "So."

"So?"

"You think I know all there is to know about you, Daniel?"

He cocked his head. "Did I leave something out?"

"I'm sure you've left out lots, but not on purpose. We certainly haven't discussed our entire lifetimes, just the high points."

"If you have questions, Maureen, ask away."

Having been given permission, she wasn't going to pass up the opportunity to ask what she'd wanted to know. "You've been single for about twenty years, right? In all that time, have you lived with a woman?"

"No."

"What's the longest relationship you've had?"

"I don't know exactly."

"Have any of them lasted a year?"

"I doubt it."

"Why is that? Boredom? Fear?"

"Yes, probably."

"Which?"

"Both." He angled closer. "The same could be said of you."

"I was getting around to that point. We're quite a pair, aren't we? Not exactly relationship champs." She turned toward her bedroom. "Good night, Daniel."

He cupped her arm, stopping her from leaving. "People change."

She climbed into bed a minute later, trying to sort out her thoughts. She'd decided weeks ago that it wasn't the attraction that mattered, but what they did about it. That being an adult meant controlling your impulses, because consequences mattered.

People change. He was right. She'd changed a little. Jess had changed a lot, but then she was at an age where change was part of life. Could Daniel change? Is that what he was saying?

Maureen closed her eyes and listened to Riley breathe. There would be time enough for decisions about Daniel.

After all, it only affected her entire future.

CHAPTER 18

Rileyism #53: "I'm sad, too."

"Gramster."

Riley's whisper in Maureen's ear tickled. "What?" she whispered back.

"It's time to get up."

She glanced at the clock—6:15 a.m.—then focused on his adorable face. He curled up against her, letting her put her arms around him. "It's early, sweetie. Everyone else is sleeping."

"I've got an idea. Let's wake 'em up."

She smiled at the ceiling. "I've got a different idea. How about if you and I get dressed and head to the PeaceLove. We'll have hot chocolate."

"O-kay!"

They were as quiet as they could manage as they dressed, then tiptoed down the hall and outside, Riley stopping his giggles with a hand over his mouth. She resisted the temptation to look into the living room as they passed by, wondering if they'd awakened Daniel but assuming he would call out to them if they had.

The morning was mild and damp, the Sunday traffic light. Maureen and Riley held hands, swinging their arms as they made their way to Cortland Avenue. As they passed the house Maureen now knew belonged to the family named Emerson who had a new baby, she wondered how Mrs. Emerson's mother was doing. Maureen would take some cookies over later and introduce herself. Maybe she could hold the baby. It would be fun to cradle a newborn again.

Then again, it may make her crave one of her own too much.

Maureen and Riley stepped inside the PeaceLove. The background music was more mellow in the morning, maybe Ravi Shankar playing his sitar? Something soothing, anyway.

"Where's your Papa, Riley?" asked the hostess.

"Sleepin'. Guess what? Me and my mom are going to Disneyland."

"Yeah? That'll be fun. Say hi to Mickey for me, okay?"

"I will," he said seriously.

They were seated and ordered hot chocolate. Maureen recalled the first time they'd come and how fascinated he'd been with the psychedelic decor and learning about hippies, and how his dear old auntie had been one. He and Cherie had put their heads together as they'd drawn on the paper tablecloth. So much had changed since then, all of it for the better.

A while later they picked out an assortment of sweets for breakfast and headed home. She slipped her key into her lock, then looked down at him. He looked back, waiting, questioning her silently.

"I'm sure going to miss you," she said, her voice hitching. She'd been so determined not to cry in front of him.

"I'll come back again real soon, okay, Gramster?"

He never called her Grandma anymore. Her nickname had stuck for good—or until he was a teenager, probably. She crouched down and drew him close for a big hug. "You're my special boy. I love you so much."

"I love you, too." He put his hands on her cheeks. "Are you sad?" he asked, touching noses.

"A little." A lot. More than a lot. He'd brought such light to her life, had shown her a different path without knowing the impact he was having.

"I'm sad, too." He wrapped his arms around her neck and buried his face against her. "You should come live with me and Mom. You could live in Papa's house. It's big."

The front door opened. Daniel was dressed for a run.

"Is this a private hug or can anyone join in?" he asked.

Riley giggled as Daniel went down on his knees and hugged them both, making growly sounds like a bear.

"You're both up bright and early." He let them go and stood, but his gaze landed on Maureen, who appreciated the tender sympathy in his eyes. He would see Riley again, probably in a couple of weeks, in time for school to start. She wouldn't, not until Christmas.

"Are Jess and Keith awake?" she asked, standing.

"Nope."

"We got goodies. Maybe I'll fix breakfast burritos."

"I think they want to get on the road pretty early."

"I'll do all the prep work now. It won't take long to put it all together as soon as they're up."

He started jogging in place. "I'll only be gone a half hour or so."

"Okay." She realized that Riley had already gone inside. She would bet that Jess and Keith would soon be awake.

"Maureen."

"Yes?"

"You'll see him again, *and* he'll remember you even more."

"I know. Separation anxiety," she said with a half smile.

He ran his fingertips down her cheek, then took off. Her skin still thrumming, she watched until he was out of sight, admiring his strong, athletic legs and long, easy stride. She loved the way his hair bounced as he moved, how the gold in it shimmered, even in the gray-sky morning.

She heard laughter from inside the house and knew that Riley had awakened Jess.

Maureen put a smile on her face, straightened her shoulders and went inside.

RILEY WAS TOO EXCITED about going to Disneyland to have another emotional farewell with Maureen. He hopped down the stairs and ran toward the car, Keith following him. Maureen had desperately wanted to have a you'd-better-take-good-care-of-my-daughter-and-grandson talk with Keith, but resisted.

Daniel made his farewells, then disappeared into the house, giving Maureen time alone with her daughter.

"I don't know Keith well, but I like him a lot," Maureen said.

"And you'll trust my judgment?"

"Yes." She set her hands on Jess's shoulders. "Oh, honey. I can't tell you what these past couple of months have meant to me."

"I can see it—in Riley, too. He's worried about you, you know. He wants you to come to Seattle and live with us."

It wasn't an invitation but a comment. Maureen let go of the breath she hadn't realized she'd been holding, waiting for Jess to turn it into an invitation. "He's a sweetie. You've done a beautiful job raising him." She pulled Jess into her arms so that she wouldn't see the tears welling. She'd wanted that invitation, wanted it desperately. "I love you, Jess. Thank you so much for the gift of Riley."

"I love you, too, Mom. Thanks for all you did for me, all my life."

"Be happy."

"I will be. I am." She leaned back and put her hands on Maureen's cheeks just as Riley had done. "I promise I'll keep in touch more."

Maureen nodded, not trusting her voice.

She followed Jess out, then stood on the sidewalk, blowing kisses with Riley, then waving until they were out of sight. She returned to the house. When the door latched behind her, the sound echoed.

She tracked down Daniel in the kitchen. "I'm glad you're here. I'm not sure I could've handled the quiet."

"He does tend to liven up a place, doesn't he?"

She smiled, not an easy thing to do. "Do you want to shower first or should I?"

"Yes."

"Yes, which?"

He took both her hands in his. "Why don't we both shower first?"

Her heart raced. "Um. You don't think we should talk about it?"

"I think we've talked about it and around it for quite a while. As you said yourself, we could easily overtalk it, and even talk ourselves out of it."

"What about the consequences? We'll be in each other's lives forever because of Riley. Should we know each other that intimately?" Why was she trying to talk him out of it? It was what she wanted, had wanted for a long time.

He pressed a kiss to the tender spot beneath her ear, then dragged his lips along her jaw. "It'll satisfy our curiosity, don't you think? We won't spend the rest of our lives wondering."

She laughed shakily. "Is that argument usually effective?"

"I've never been faced with this particular issue before. I'm feeling my way through it." He followed up his words by sliding his hands down her arms then slipping them around her waist. He tugged her against him, then curved his hands over her rear, holding her still. "You're curious, aren't you?"

"Beyond curious," she answered honestly. "It's become a need."

"One you would've resisted if I hadn't made the first move?"

"I don't know. Probably not."

"Discussion over, then." He took her hand and walked through the house and into the bathroom. He started the shower, waited for the water to warm, adjusted the faucets to the perfect temperature, then turned to her. He kicked off his sneakers, tossed his socks aside.

She peeled his T-shirt over his head, then dropped it on the vanity. Her hands shook as she dragged her fingertips down his chest lightly, slowly, exploring the ridges and planes, then hooking the elastic waist of his shorts. He ducked his head and found her lips with his, pressing hers open. He swung her around and moved her against the wall, plundering with his mouth now. She took everything he had to offer and gave just as much back. Oh, the pleasure of him, of his mouth and hands. Of his body pressing into her.

She dragged his shorts down and off. Naked, he moved his hips against hers, slipped his hands between them to unbutton her blouse and peel it away. Soon she was naked, too, in the small, steam-filled room.

He finally lifted his head and took a good, long look at her. "You're everything I imagined."

She saw appreciation in his eyes and felt it in his touch as he pulled her into the shower with him. And what a shower it was, probably the longest, most thorough ever. And when they landed on her bed later after barely drying off, it was to a driving need, equally demanding and powerful....

And then, utter satisfaction.

EVENTUALLY THEIR BODY HEAT cooled and they slid under the blankets.

"Wow," Daniel said as she settled next to him. His arms came around her and she slipped a leg between his.

"Yeah." Big wow. Big finish.

Sunny said Daniel was the best she'd ever had. The words popped into her head.

Sunny hadn't exaggerated.

Maureen ignored the pangs of jealousy that threatened to diminish the experience. She needed to live in the moment. No expectations. No demands.

"Six years of foreplay. I never thought the day would come," he said against her wet hair.

"You've really wanted me all that time?"

"Yeah. I remember the first time I saw you, here, at your house. You wore a red T-shirt and black jeans. Now and then your nipples would get hard. I was sitting on your couch and you brought me a glass of iced tea." He cupped her breast and thumbed her nipple, making her arch into him and suck in a quick breath. "I wanted to pull you into my lap and taste you."

He followed up the exciting words by sliding down and taking her nipple into his mouth, his tongue rolling the hard flesh, his hand cupping and stroking her breast. She tipped back her head, her mouth open, and urged him to the other breast. The way he used his teeth and tongue and lips…

She luxuriated in his touch and his own obvious pleasure at what he was doing to her. She reached down to surround him with her hand and circle her thumb over the warm, wet tip of him. After a minute he groaned and moved atop her, slipping inside, then going absolutely still. She squeezed him tight. He let out a long, deep sound that excited her even more.

"I don't have another condom," he said, low and harsh. "Need to go to the other bedroom."

She gestured to her right. "Bedside drawer."

He managed to move her along with him without losing the connection, making her laugh. And then he kissed her, stealing the laughter, replacing it with sighs and moans, then finally demands. She'd never begged before, but she begged him now. He delayed until nothing would stop her from coming. Then he joined her.

THEY LOAFED IN BED, even eating lunch there. She slipped into one of her new nightgowns, black and lacy and revealing, and she loved the way he kept running his fingers along the low neckline, dipping beneath the fabric now and then, nipping her through the lace with his teeth, distracting her from any detailed discussion for quite a while.

"What do you remember about the day we met?" he asked finally, sitting against the headboard.

"I thought you were very sad, but of course you had reason to be. Josh had died a month before."

"What else?"

She tried to remember. "I don't know. I had no reason to be angry with you at that point, since you hadn't yet taken Jess and Riley away."

"You must've had some impression."

"I thought you were attractive and well-spoken and liberal. That long hair, you know."

He smiled. "Says a San Franciscan?"

She shrugged.

"And you never were attracted to me over the years?" he pushed.

"I didn't say that. I was aware that there was something about you that pulled me, but I was too angry and hurt to see it for anything other than what I'd lost because of you."

"I wanted you every time I saw you."

"You had a strange way of showing it."

"What was I supposed to do—come on to you? I got hard around you a lot. I'm surprised you never noticed."

"So am I, given your…proportions," she said, grinning.

"I spent a lot of time with my back turned to you."

"Oh, so that was why. I figured you couldn't stand to look at me."

He angled her away from him, then started massaging her shoulders. She dropped her chin to her chest. "You're spoiling me."

"I like touching you."

She closed her eyes, savoring the attention.

"Are you going to go back to work tomorrow or take off the whole two weeks?" he asked.

"Take the two weeks. Is that okay with you? Can you work with me around all day?"

"Employees are required to take a break every few hours."

"And I always follow the rules," she said.

"First time I can say I'm happy about that."

The phone rang, a jarring sound in their new, sheltered world.

Daniel picked up the phone and passed it to her. "Hello?"

"Hi, Mom!"

Maureen glanced at the clock. They shouldn't be in Los Angeles yet. Had the car broken down? "What's wrong?"

"Nothing. I need to talk to you about you and Daniel."

Maureen glanced at him. He raised his brows.

"I've been doing a lot of thinking as we've been driving, and I just want you to know that it's okay with me."

"What's okay with you?"

"You and Daniel. You know, as a couple. Or sleepover partners. Or whatever it is you've got going. Life's short. You should have fun whenever you can."

"Okay. Where are you?"

"I don't know. Hang on. Where are we, Keith?"

"Just over the Grapevine. About an hour to go."

"Did you hear that?"

"Yes. How's Riley doing?"

"Totally immersed in the Game Boy you gave him. I'll give you a call later, okay?"

"Sure. Have fun, honey." Maureen handed the phone back to Daniel.

"What was that about?" he asked.

"Um. I think she just gave us her blessing."

They stared at each other. She wondered what he thought, but didn't want to ask him how he felt about it, not wanting to tempt fate. But she knew what *she* felt.

Pressure.

CHAPTER 19

For the next week Maureen and Daniel worked and played and made love. It was the closest thing to a honeymoon she'd had. He was so easy to be with, so comfortable, and the most playful man she'd known. He fit, as if he'd always been there, always belonged. Sharing space with him was easy. Sleeping next to him didn't take any getting used to.

They went for walks and drives and to the movies. They held hands in public. Kissed. Hugged. She found freedom with him. And in another week it would end. He would have to report to the university. Then what?

They didn't talk about it. She didn't even want to think about it.

On Saturday Maureen went with Cherie to deliver meals while Daniel stayed home to work. He hadn't been neglecting the job, but he could get a lot more done if she wasn't around as a distraction—or so he said.

"There are stars in your eyes," Cherie said the moment she climbed into Maureen's car.

"Don't worry. I can still see clearly."

"I guess I don't have to ask who put them there."

Maureen eased into traffic. "You can probably figure it out." After a couple minutes of silence, she glanced at her aunt. "Why so quiet? It's what you wanted, isn't it? For me to have stars in my eyes?"

"You're so vulnerable right now, adorable girl."

"I'm happy, but I'm also realistic. It's a fling."

"That's not like you."

"People change." Maureen remembered when Daniel had said that. While she believed it to a point, she knew that most people didn't make 180-degree changes, and Daniel making a commitment to a woman would be just that. "Can we talk about something else, please? How's Bonnie doing? Her husband had to report back to his ship yesterday, right?"

"He did. And Jeremy also convinced her to move home to be near her mother for the rest of his tour."

"Really? That's great. She's from Iowa, right?"

"Ames. I told her I'd fly out with her, help her with Morgan and the baby. It's tough to travel with two little ones."

"That's very thoughtful of you." And a little amazing. Maureen couldn't remember the last time Cherie had taken any time away from her many volunteer jobs. "When are you leaving?"

"Tomorrow. Jeremy arranged for the movers."

"How long will you be gone?"

"I haven't decided. I might just take a little side trip to Chicago. Go visit an old friend."

Maureen pulled into the alley behind Manny's Stewpot

restaurant, today's provider of meals, coming to a stop by the back door. "I don't remember you talking about an old friend from Chicago."

Cherie fidgeted. Cherie *never* fidgeted.

"I told you about him recently," she said, looking out the window.

"Him? Him who? Oh! The man you loved but didn't think you were good enough for?"

"Max. He was widowed last year."

"How'd you find him?"

"He found me a couple of months ago. We've been talking."

Maureen finally saw how giddy Cherie looked. There were stars in *her* eyes. "How long has it been since you've seen him?"

"I don't know exactly."

Maureen raised her brows.

"Okay. About thirty-four years. And three months. And four days."

"But you don't know exactly."

"Well, not to the minute."

Maureen did the math in her head. That would've been when her mother died and Cherie came to live with her and her father. Is that what had stopped Cherie from being with Max, not her excuse that she didn't think she was good enough for him? It would be just like Cherie to tell that kind of fib so that Maureen wouldn't feel guilty.

She hugged her aunt long and hard. "I hope he hasn't changed."

"I hope he's aged! Otherwise what would he do with the likes of me?"

They smiled at each other.

"Would you move there?" Maureen asked after they climbed out of the car and headed to the back door of the restaurant.

"I don't want to tempt fate by thinking about it. And, you know, I've got so much going here."

"Is that why you were pushing me at Dad so hard? You might move and we'd be left without you to mediate?"

"Partly. Although I wish I'd done that years ago."

"Things happen as they're supposed to." She held the door for her aunt then followed her into the restaurant kitchen, where they were greeted like family. She would continue this work for Cherie, Maureen decided, continue the legacy. It was the least she could do for the woman who may not have given birth to her, but who had shown her how to live.

MONDAY MORNING CAME too fast. Maureen and Daniel's week in Eden was over, and she had to return to work. He was done with his project, as well. Until he had feedback on the first one, he wouldn't start on another.

Maureen awoke, for the first time not feeling him spooned along her back, his arms around her. She rolled over. He was sitting against the headboard, dressed in running shorts and T-shirt.

"Awake at last," he said, looking...nervous? Distant?

"Am I late?" She couldn't see the clock with him in the way.

"Not even close."

She pushed herself up, resting against the headboard, too, keeping the blanket over her bare body since he looked so serious, when what she wanted to do was kiss him until he forgot whatever it was that was bothering him. "I really don't want to go to work," she said.

"It was a good week."

The tiniest bit of panic set in at his tone of voice, which sounded almost as if he was saying this was the end, right now. *We still have one more*, she wanted to shout. Instead, she managed to say it calmly. "We have another week until you have to report to work."

"Then what?"

She couldn't read his expression at all. "I don't know what you're asking, Daniel."

"When will we see each other again?"

You want to see me again? "Christmas, for sure. I'll fly up."

"Not good enough." He didn't touch her, didn't give her a clue about how he felt. Only his words indicated he'd been thinking about their relationship.

"Do you have some suggestions?" she asked.

"I think you should move to Seattle."

It wasn't as if the idea hadn't occurred to her, especially now that her relationship with Jess and Riley was so strong. But there was a lot to keep her in San Francisco. She'd just committed herself to carrying on Cherie's work if she moved—

"Live with me," he added, quiet but intense.

What? Live with him? *What?*

"I see I've shocked you."

"Well…yes. You told me you've never lived with a woman since your divorce."

"True."

"Why me? Why now?"

"I don't want what we have to end."

She'd never had anyone look at her the way he was, as if trying to see all the way into the core of her brain.

"It would be good, Maureen. You would be next door to Jess and Riley. They would have the benefit of having both of us nearby. You could get a new job. You said you figure you'll be stuck in the one you have forever. This would force a change. And you know if we try to keep a long-distance relationship going, it's probably not going to work. They rarely do."

She studied his eyes, saw something she'd never seen before, something she couldn't interpret. Finally she tugged the blanket a little higher, tucking it under her chin. "I can't have this discussion while I'm naked."

He leaned across her and grabbed her robe off the floor. She slipped into it. Now what she needed was time. She couldn't make that kind of decision with the snap of her fingers.

"I can't believe you haven't thought about it," he said.

"I've been trying to live in the moment instead of planning ahead as I've always done." And, frankly, he wasn't acting loverlike, but as if this was a business proposition of some sort—friends with benefits. She wanted to see passion in his eyes about her moving in with him. And *need*.

The potential repercussions could be huge for her. She'd been falling in love with him, she could admit that. But she also knew he was a big risk. His track record proved that.

"I'm going for a run," he said. "When you get home from work tonight, we'll talk."

She nodded. Anything to buy her time. "You know I'll probably be working late, maybe until eight, the way I did before Riley came."

"Okay." He kissed her, gently, sweetly, but didn't plead his cause further.

She didn't move until after she heard the front door shut, then, before she could just pull the blankets over her head and analyze her situation ad nauseum, she climbed in the shower and got ready for work. Moving to Seattle would be good for her relationship with Jess and Riley. And good for *her*. She *had* stayed in her job and her house for all these years because it was safe—and because it had given Jess a place to come home to.

But Jess wasn't coming home, ever. Maybe she would come for more frequent visits now, but never again to live. Jess was also at a turning point in her life.

So, what had stopped Maureen from saying yes instantly?

Because Daniel had made it clear that he didn't want to get married again—ever—and he didn't want to have another child, both things she wanted.

He hadn't said he loved her.

The answer should be simple—one-word simple: *no*.

But her heart threatened to make it a whole lot more complicated.

EVERYONE AT PRIMERO greeted Maureen as if she'd been gone for months. The tension didn't seem as thick as when she'd left for vacation, maybe because ShortTakes would debut this week, hitting the chain-bookstore and student-bookstore shelves right on schedule, just in time for the new school year.

Anza stood in her office doorway to greet her. "Well, don't you look sexy and sassy."

So much had happened in the past week, she'd forgotten about her minimakeover. "You like it?"

"Looking fine, indeed. We'll have lunch, okay? Looks like we have things to talk about."

"Sure."

"Bernadette wanted to see you the minute you arrived."

Maureen pulled a folder from her briefcase and passed it to Anza. "Here's the final draft on *Twelfth Night*. Let me know what you think."

She headed down the hall and around the corner to Bernadette's office. Everything seemed surreal. Daniel had asked her to move in with him. Nothing beyond that one sentence stayed in her thoughts for long.

"Have a seat," Bernadette said, looking more rested than Maureen had seen her for a long time. "Obviously, a vacation was exactly what the doctor ordered. You look terrific."

"I could say the same about you."

"I'm seeing a grief counselor. It's helping. I don't think the office is set to mutiny anymore."

"Everyone understands what you've been going through, Bernadette. But I think it's wonderful that you're getting help and feeling better."

"Thanks. And thanks for being my number-one supporter all along. It meant a lot."

"You and Carlos changed my life. Friends stand by each other."

"Ready to get back to work?"

No. She wished she could be honest and just say it. "I just gave Anza Daniel Cregg's final on *Twelfth Night.*"

"Good. I'll be interested in her opinion. Did he enjoy working on the project?"

Maureen wasn't quite sure how to answer that. "He enjoyed the challenge very much." Just not the purpose, she thought with a smile.

"Well, I have some news for you. Doug has decided against taking the VP job. He's moving his family to Arizona because his youngest needs a drier climate. I'm offering the position to you."

Maureen sat back, stunned.

"Welcome back," Bernadette said, her smile like that of the old days when work was fun.

"I don't know what to say," Maureen said finally. "I need to think about it."

She had shocked Bernadette, that much was obvious.

She'd even shocked herself, which made her think she'd made up her mind about going to Seattle. She wanted so much to be close to her daughter and grandson. And a new job in a new city *would* shake up her life. Turning forty seemed to be the right time for a big change.

But she needed more of a commitment from Daniel before she moved into his house—and she didn't think he wanted to make that commitment.

Too much to think about all at once. Bernadette told her to take her time, but was still clearly surprised. Maureen went to her own office in a daze and shut the door. She sank into her chair, ignored the stack of folders in her In Box and stared at her San Francisco-skyline poster.

After a minute she took a legal pad from her desk drawer and started three pro-and-con lists: Move to Seattle, Move in with Daniel and Take the Promotion. Her pen hovered over the paper for long seconds, then she wadded it up and tossed it into the wastepaper basket.

She wanted to go with her gut, to live in the moment. She wanted to do what *felt* right, not just what made the most sense. She didn't want lists to determine her choice.

After a while she canceled her lunch with Anza. She would've called Cherie and asked for advice, but Cherie was gone, and, anyway, this time Maureen needed to make her own decisions. So, during her lunch break, she contacted a Seattle headhunter about the job market and was given a great deal of hope that her skills would result in only brief unemployment. That much she needed to know in order to make such a huge life change. There had to be good, interesting work for her.

Then she sat at her desk, her head in her hands, her future in turmoil, when her phone rang.

"Hi, Mom, guess what?"

"I have no idea."

"I'm getting married!"

"Wha—" She sat straight up. "Married? Now?"

"Not right this second." She laughed. "I want a real wedding, and that takes time. But we're going to move to L.A. before Riley's school year starts, then probably get married around Christmas."

Move to L.A.? Now? Just when Maureen had almost decided to move to Seattle?

"That's…great, honey. Great."

"Please don't be upset. I can tell you're not sure about Keith, but he's the right one, Mom. And Riley adores him."

"It's not Keith in particular, but getting married so fast, that's all. What's the rush?"

"We love each other. We don't want to wait."

Pressure had been building in Maureen's chest, hot and heavy. She finally broke down. Her baby was getting married. "I'm happy for you, honey," she said, choking on tears.

"I can tell!"

"Have you told Daniel?"

"Of course not. I wanted to tell you first. Um, maybe you'd like to tell him?"

Meaning, Jess didn't want to break that particular news. "If you want."

"That would be great. Then I'll talk to him afterward. I think he's going to take it hard, having Riley and me move away."

"I imagine so." Maureen was glad Jess hadn't known what Daniel had proposed.

"Maybe I should tell you my other news, Mom. I was going to wait, but…"

Was she pregnant? No, she couldn't be. Or at least she couldn't know that yet. "Don't keep me in suspense."

"I'm going to be a stuntwoman!"

Maureen closed her eyes and stifled a groan. Her daughter may have matured a lot because of her *True Grit* experience, but she was as impulsive as ever.

"Is there some special training for that?" Maureen asked her daughter.

"Sure, lots. But Keith'll make sure I get the best."

Uh-oh. No hope, then, of Keith talking her out of her decision. "I see."

"I gotta run. We'll talk later, okay? Bye."

Well. Just how much life altering was one woman supposed to handle in one day, anyway? She felt stressed to maximum breaking point.

Finally, in a daze, she grabbed her briefcase, told Anza she was sick and was going home then walked to her boss's office.

"I need to go home," Maureen said, her throat closing.

Bernadette got out of her chair and came around the desk. "What's wrong?"

"I'll tell you tomorrow, okay?" She needed to go right now.

Bernadette touched her arm. The sympathetic gesture spurred Maureen out of the room.

She took the bus home but didn't go in her house. Instead she retrieved her car. Her primary reason for moving to Seattle was gone. Now what? Should she stay in San Francisco, closer to L.A., where she could spend weekends more easily? Or should she move to Seattle, anyway, to be with Daniel? Would he still want her there, without Jess and Riley?

Maureen had choices. Too many choices, even including moving to L.A. herself, to be near Jess and Riley. Yet another possibility to toss into the decision pool.

The choices swirled in her head as she drove across the Golden Gate and up into the Marin headlands to her favorite place.

She wouldn't leave until she'd made up her mind.

"YOU'RE HOME EARLY," Daniel said two hours later when she tracked him down in the kitchen. He was stirring something in a big pot, just like that first day two months ago. The memory was so clear and sharp, she could almost see Riley standing on a chair at the sink, washing the lettuce.

She knew Daniel intimately now. She had the right to touch him, to thread her fingers through his soft, thick hair, to run her tongue down his bare flesh, to lean against him as they watched television, her head nestled in that cozy spot on his chest. He'd become a partner, truly a partner. She hadn't known what she'd been missing until she had it—with him.

He came across the kitchen, looking concerned. She resisted the temptation to take a step back. "I told them I was sick and needed to go home," she said before he could kiss her. She needed distance for this discussion.

He put a hand on her forehead. She closed her eyes. "Why don't you stretch out on the couch? Can I get you something? Water? Tea?"

She shook her head. "We need to talk. I'll feel better after we talk."

He held her gaze a little while. His eyes dulled, as if preparing himself for the worst, then he turned off the flame under the pot and gestured for her to lead the way. They sat at opposite ends of the sofa.

"Bernadette offered me the vice presidency today."

A few beats passed. "Congratulations?"

She heard the question in his voice. "I haven't accepted."

"Okay."

"Then Jess called. She's getting married—around Christmas, she thinks. She's moving to L.A. now, however."

He looked away, but not before she saw how shaken he was. Apparently, like her, he hadn't seriously considered the possibility. They should have.

"*And* she says she's becoming a stuntwoman."

Daniel tipped back his head and dragged his hands down his face. "I guess that shouldn't really come as a surprise, either."

"Why?"

"Keith's father is one of the most renown stuntmen in Hollywood. Keith has been in the business himself since he was a teenager."

"How do you know that?"

"He told me. He didn't want me to worry about Jess."

"I don't understand why *she* didn't want to tell us."

"You know Jess," Daniel said. "Loves the big surprise."

"And what's your excuse?"

"For what?"

"For not telling me about Keith, Daniel. Why didn't you relieve me of my worries about Jess?"

He frowned. "It was Jess's place to tell you. Obviously she wanted to do it in her own time."

It was a small issue in the grand scheme of things, Maureen decided. And he was right—it was Jess's news to share, not his.

"It changes things, doesn't it?" he asked. "Having Jess and Riley move from Seattle changes everything."

She gathered her thoughts. After a long hesitation, she said, "On the Marin side of the Golden Gate, there's a place I go when I need to make a decision or come to terms with a problem I'm facing. I sit on the ground and watch the Bay and the skyline. The wind blows my hair and helps clear my thoughts. I don't know why, but it's been a magical place for me through the years. I've never left there without having made a big decision—until today. I don't have answers yet, Daniel."

He crossed his arms and stared at the window for quite a while before he said, "When you didn't say yes this morning, when you had to think about it, I figured you'd already made your decision. If you'd wanted to be with me, you would've said yes."

"Even before being offered the promotion and hearing Jess's news, it wasn't that yes-or-no simple, Daniel."

"And now it's more complicated because your most important reason for moving to Seattle is no longer even in play. Being with me isn't enough to make you move."

He didn't sound hurt, but matter-of-fact. "You aren't considering moving to L.A.?" she asked.

"To change teaching positions at this point would be foolhardy. I'm in line to be department chair within the next couple of years. And except for Jess and Riley living there, southern California holds no appeal to me whatsoever. I like Seattle. I've made a home there…. Are you thinking of following them?"

"It's a possibility." She wished she could read his mind—or at least his expression. He certainly wasn't begging her to move to Seattle. It was almost as if he'd accepted that she wasn't coming and had already moved on. "I need more time to sort out all the issues."

"Maureen, if you need more time, you don't have a strong need to do one thing in particular, so maybe you should just leave things as they are. I can't move. I suspect you're in the same boat, professionally."

"There's more here for me than just my job," she countered, feeling cold suddenly.

He stood. "I'm going to check on flights home."

Maureen was staggered by how easily he'd given up. *This* man she recognized from the past six years. So, okay, he might not be ordering her to move to Seattle or else, but he wasn't dangling a lure, as he had to Jess years ago. Still, he was the man who, once he made up his mind, felt it was his way or no way. Obviously he didn't care enough to work with her on a solution beneficial to both of them—all of them.

So much for the new-found partnership.

So much for…love. She squeezed her eyes shut. She'd fallen for him, although at this point she wondered why.

Oh, but when he was playful and loving and sexy…she knew why then.

Maureen sat and waited, her thoughts scattered and torn. The burden of all the sudden changes and decisions was bad enough, but the fact he'd changed his mind so quickly said everything. He couldn't have been that emotionally involved, after all. She didn't understand why he'd even asked her to move in.

When he reemerged, he carried his suitcases. "I called a cab. There's a flight in three hours."

Shutting down her emotions and responding in kind, she approached him. "I don't know why you're so angry, Daniel.

You asked me to move in with you. Given that you haven't lived with any woman, or even spent a whole year in a relationship, makes it hard for me to say yes. I could be giving up everything only to have it cave in on me after I've changed my whole life. Quit my job. Sold my house."

"Are you looking for some kind of commitment from me?"

"You think I should make that kind of move without one? Tell me why I should." *I dare you. I double-dog dare you.*

A horn honked. His cab had arrived.

Neither of them looked away.

"The fact I asked should have told you everything," he said. Then he picked up his suitcases and headed for the front door.

No, it doesn't. I need the words. She swallowed hard. "I guess it'll be easy enough to avoid each other now that Jess and Riley won't be living with you," she said. "But we will have to work together until George can take over again. Can you do that?"

"Sure, no problem. Can you?"

"No problem here, either."

He opened the front door and waved at the cabbie, then he turned and looked at her. "Bye, Maureen."

She raised her hand slightly.

And then he was gone, walking out of her house as easily as he'd walked in, but leaving her changed in the process. She should thank him for that much, for his part in the positive changes he'd inspired.

But for the life of her, she couldn't form a word.

CHAPTER 20

On a September day a month later, Maureen paced her office, looking at the clock every few seconds. It was the first time she'd invited her father to have lunch with her, and he was late. He was never late. She'd never thought retirement could change a man so set in his ways, but apparently it had. And he'd only been retired for a week, a quick, recent decision.

Her intercom buzzed. "Your father is here," the receptionist said.

"Thanks. I'll be right out."

She brushed her hands down her jacket and headed to the lobby.

She smiled when she saw him, his posture as ramrod straight as ever, but a definite softening in his face. He looked...relaxed.

"Hi, Dad."

They hugged easily, now. Comfortably.

"I never knew what kind of environment you worked in. Now I know. Now I can picture it. It's nice."

The brick walls were a perfect backdrop for the large

posters of many of Primero's book jackets, showing a cross-section of their nonfiction publications.

"I just read that one," Bill said, pointing at the poster of *Retirement Isn't for Sissies*.

"Did you enjoy it?" She headed toward her office, and he followed along.

"I thought he had a lot of good ideas."

"Will you be happy in retirement, do you think?"

"I need to keep busy. Norma and I bought a motor home. We're going to see America."

"Really? That's great. When do you leave?" They arrived at her office.

"After the wedding— Well, I'll be. Look at that plaque on the door. You got yourself promoted. A vice president, no less." Pride shimmered in him. "When did that happen?"

"A month ago, but the sign was just put up yesterday. I didn't tell you earlier because I wanted it to be a surprise. For you to see it for yourself."

"It's a good one."

"Imagine, Dad," she said quietly, hooking her arm through his and leaning against him. "The girl without a high school diploma, a single mom at seventeen, and here I am, vice president of a growing, successful publishing house."

ShortTakes were doing well so far. The Goof-Proof Guides had just hit the stores and were getting good press.

"You've worked hard for it, Mo."

"You taught me that."

Her words pleased him, she could see. They moved into

her office so that she could get her purse. The late-September day was warm enough that she didn't need a sweater. They would walk to her favorite taqueria.

"How are the wedding plans going?" he asked as they kept pace.

"Cherie is giddy. She and Max put an offer on a house this morning not far from where she lives now. It's much bigger. Since he's got three sons scattered around the country, each with children, they want a big enough space for everyone to visit."

"I'm headed over to meet him as soon as I leave you."

"You'll like him. He absolutely adores her, and she's like a schoolgirl. He wants her to continue her 'good works,' as he calls them, but he also wants to take her around the world. I think he's convinced her."

"And you, Mo? How's your personal life? I kind of thought for a while there that you and Daniel might hook up. Cherie hinted at it."

"I haven't seen or talked to him in a month. We e-mailed a couple of times because of some business with Primero, but the person who was promoted into my position is in charge of the authors now, so she has contact with him, not me."

"Which doesn't answer my question."

They went into the restaurant and found a table. Only after they'd ordered did their conversation start again. "So?" he pushed.

"So, yes, there had seemed to be a possibility of something happening, but it fell apart. His choice. He ended it. I'm over it."

He drilled her with his eyes.

"I am, Dad." Except that every so often she would see a man leaning against a doorjamb, a typical pose for Daniel, or out for a run on her street, or sitting in the PeaceLove, and think it was him. Her heart would beat a quicker cadence, then she would realize it was only her imagination playing tricks.

His loss, she told herself constantly. His big, fat loss.

But my hurt. She'd been angry at first, then she'd come to realize he'd probably been mourning the loss of Jess and Riley. She'd thought with time he would recover, be in touch with her. It hadn't happened.

"So," Maureen said, deciding to change the subject. "If you're leaving after Cherie's wedding, what about Jess's big Hollywood party on Thanksgiving weekend for the final episode of *True Grit?* I thought you and Norma were going to attend."

"We need to get ahead of the weather if we want to get to Boston before the snow starts in the plains. We'll watch the program from the road and give her a call. We won't even know if she's in the top two until the week before, right? Do you think she won?"

"I have no clue. Does that mean you won't be here for Jess and Keith's wedding in December?"

"Wouldn't miss it. We'll fly in from wherever we are."

"Oh, good. Jess would've been very disappointed."

After a while their food was served. They dug in for few minutes, then her father said casually, "Saw Ted the other day."

She looked at him, wordless, her fork in midair.

"He's looking well."

She continued to stare in silence, but took a bite of her enchilada.

"Well, I always liked him."

"I know you did, Dad."

"He asked about you."

"To which you said?"

"That you were fine. Still single."

Suspicious, Maureen asked, "And how did you happen to see Ted? I can't imagine your paths crossing accidentally."

Bill shrugged. "He called. Took me to lunch."

"You are not to repeat to him anything we discuss, understand?" She loved adding the "understand" to the sentence after all those years of him using it. "I would appreciate it if you would turn down further invitations from him."

"But if you married Ted I would have no reason to worry about you. That Daniel, he was a wild one sometimes, I hear."

In the best possible way....

"Ted and Daniel were about as opposite as they could get, Dad. That's neither good nor bad. It just *is*. Why are you pushing about this when I've asked you to leave it alone?"

"I'm curious."

She hadn't known him to be a curious man. "Well, I'm your daughter, and your loyalty should be to me."

"Okay, okay. I do wonder, though, how you can avoid seeing Daniel. There's the *True Grit* party in November and Jess's wedding in December. I expect he'll be at both."

"He'll be at the wedding—" *which gives me three more months, so I'll be fine* "—but Jess says he always goes away for Thanksgiving. Some friend's cabin. It's a buddy thing, many years of tradition. He never misses it." The wedding was a long way off.

"Before I forget, Norma wants to know if you have any ideas about a wedding gift for Cherie and Max."

"A donation to Mobile Meals to help pay for transportation expenses."

"But that's—"

"Exactly what she wants. And that's an order."

OCTOBER CAME, and with it the unmatched beauty of fall in San Francisco, with its clear skies and perfect temperature. Maureen watched Max take Cherie onto the dance floor for the first time as his wife. The party was small, only fifty people, and the wedding had been beautiful, taking place in an old chapel in Marin, with beautiful stained-glass windows. And now the reception at a Sausalito restaurant with a view of the Bay and the city across from it.

"Hi, Gramster."

Maureen pushed back from the table to let Riley climb into her lap. She hugged him mightily. "This is fun, hmm?"

"Yeah. Auntie Cherie smiles, smiles, smiles."

"She sure does. I'm so glad you're here. I've missed you sooo much."

"Me, too. An' I miss Papa."

"I know. You like Keith a lot, right?"

He became instantly animated. "He's hecka fun! We get to go to movie sets. It's awesome. I hafta stay real quiet."

Maureen could hardly imagine it.

Jess came over and sat in the chair vacated by Cherie. "You look fabulous, Mom. That's a gorgeous maid-of-honor dress, and the turquoise color is perfect on you. You've lost weight, haven't you?"

"A little." For a while after Daniel left she hadn't been hungry, then, mad at herself for letting him affect her so much, she'd forced herself not just to eat again but to get out into the world more. Weekends, she walked. She went out to restaurants alone and struck up conversations. She'd met some fascinating people, and was enjoying her life more. They were back to working ten-hour days at Primero instead of twelve, and the difference felt huge. She had lots of time on her hands and was learning to fill it.

"So…" Maureen said to her daughter. "It's pretty fascinating watching you week to week on *True Grit*. Sometimes I hardly recognize you."

"We all became different people. You have to think like a teammate, but look out for your own interests. It's a fine line to walk."

"I can see that."

"I'll bet you've squirmed now and then." Jess grinned.

Having Riley in her lap prevented Maureen from making any pointed remarks about how much she'd learned about her daughter that surprised her. "I'm proud of you and very impressed. You're in the final four. That's incredible!"

Jess hugged her.

"What do you hear from Daniel?" Maureen asked casually.

"He's been pretty quiet."

Still in mourning? Maureen wondered. She'd felt an incredible amount of sympathy for him, having lost Jess and Riley herself at one time, but as time passed...

"May I have this dance?" she asked her sweet grandson, who had nestled comfortably against her.

"All right!"

Maureen drank champagne and danced the night away, abandoning her shoes early on, abandoning her inhibitions a little later, but not enough to embarrass herself. She had fun. She felt great. Life was good.

At the end of the evening, the single women gathered to catch the bouquet. Jess dragged her into the small group but positioned herself at the front. She wasn't taking any chances that her wedding wouldn't happen. A little good-natured elbowing ensued.

Cherie tossed the bouquet. Jess leaped. Grabbed it by the blooms. Lost it.

And it fell directly into Maureen's hands.

Everyone applauded. Jess plunked her fists on her hips and pretended to scowl.

Maureen taunted her daughter jokingly, but inside, deep inside, she hurt.

WHAT A DIFFERENCE a month made. The last time Maureen had seen Jess was at Cherie's wedding, a small, elegant affair. Tonight she was in a screening room in someone's mansion. In Hollywood.

She looked around in wonder at the people waiting for the showing of the *True Grit* finale. It wasn't a who's-who-in-Hollywood group of people in terms of star power, but Jess had run down the guest list with Maureen, telling her who each person was. Movers and shakers, mostly behind the scenes, a different kind of star power.

It had been a four-day whirlwind for Maureen—Thanksgiving Day with Keith's family, whom she liked very much. His parents had been married for thirty-five years, amazing for Hollywood. He had two brothers and two sisters, lots of nieces and nephews. Jess and Riley merged and mingled easily with all of them, the kind of family life Maureen wished she'd given her.

She met other interesting people all weekend, too, even some men her age, attentive and interested. Jess cautioned her about each of them. Maureen just enjoyed the flattery.

The lights dimmed and the program began, projected on a movie-theater-size screen for the hundred people invited. It was a two-hour show, but without commercials, much shorter. Jess and one other contestant, Dante Ito, had made it to the finals. Maureen was filled with pride.

Most of the show was a retelling of the previous eleven

weeks, although with new footage. No matter the outcome, Jess was a winner. She'd worked hard but kept her sense of humor and her innate kindness. The other contestants liked her. Dante Ito was popular, too, and a little more driven.

During intermission, Maureen went to the bathroom then grabbed a glass of champagne to take back into the theater with her. She watched Riley flit from person to person, a social butterfly. It was a good fit for him, she realized. All this activity and action was what he needed as an outlet for his natural exuberance. And Jess shone. Her new maturity was evident, her happiness even more so.

"She looks blissful."

Maureen froze at the words. Daniel. There. Beside her. She didn't want to look at him. She had to look at him.

"Yes," she said, turning toward him. "She's happy."

He, on the other hand, looked…not happy. He'd lost his tan, lost some weight, lost the twinkle in his eyes.

"You look incredible," he said, lifting a hand toward her, then dropping it.

Her heart pounded in her ears, loud and fast. "I thought you weren't coming, Daniel." *Keep cool. Keep cool.*

"I left the cabin early today and caught a flight. It was driving me crazy not being here, not seeing them…."

Yes, he had been in mourning. Deep mourning. Almost like losing his son again, Maureen thought. She wanted to take him in her arms and comfort him. Instead, she touched her hand to his. He grabbed hers and held tight.

"I see you everywhere, Maureen." His voice was raw.

She didn't even have to ask what he meant. She knew. Just as she saw him in men who leaned against doorjambs or whenever a jogger ran by on her street, she knew.

"I've missed you," he said simply.

It's going to be okay, she thought, unable to speak. It's all going to turn out.

"Okay, everyone. Let's see how this ends," Keith shouted, directing them back into the theater.

Without words Maureen and Daniel moved into the theater together and took seats beside each other, next to Jess and Riley, who leaped into Daniel's arms and buried his face as Jess looked on, smiling, apparently not surprised.

"Papa! Papa! I knew you'd come. I knew it."

Riley sat in Daniel's lap. Maureen was aware of him every second. Their arms brushed occasionally. She swore she could hear him breathing, even though the background music was too loud to hear anyone breathe.

Riley moved to sit with Jess as the winner was about to be announced. Daniel reached for Maureen's hand.

"The clan has decided. Our winner is…Dante Ito."

Noises of protest filled the room. Jess laughed. As the second-place winner, she'd won a hundred thousand dollars. But, even better, she announced to the room of people, she'd found Keith. *She* was the big winner.

Time passed like slow-motion film to Maureen. Buffet tables of food were devoured. Wine and champagne flowed. Jess took Daniel around the room, introducing him, as Maureen watched, confused and cautious.

When the crowd thinned, Riley seemed glued to Daniel. He lifted Riley into his arms and hugged him, his eyes closed. He'd denied himself his grandson for three months. Maureen hadn't. She'd seen him at least once a month, and would continue to keep close contact. The computer and telephone could only do so much.

But he would know now not to deny himself. And he'd held her hand and told her he missed her....

Jess came up to her.

"Are you worn out?" Maureen asked, slipping her arm around her daughter's waist.

"Running on adrenaline."

"I'm so proud of you, honey."

"Thanks, Mom." She gestured toward Daniel and Riley. "Were you surprised to see him?"

"Definitely. How come you didn't tell me?" Why hadn't he come back to her? Talked to her?

"It was a night for surprises, don't you think?"

Maureen smiled. "How soon until we leave?"

"Ten minutes, probably." She waved at someone. "I need to go—"

"Of course." Maureen was waiting for Daniel, anyway.

He finally approached. "Hi."

"Hi, yourself." She waited for him to pick up where he'd left off. *I've missed you....*

"How's the new job working out?" he asked when she said nothing.

Job? Who cared? "It's fine. Everything has finally settled

down. Bernadette took some time off, plus she hired a couple of new staffers. Everyone is happy again." She was babbling. "How's yours?"

"Same old, same old. Are you flying home tonight?"

"Tomorrow morning. I took the day off, decided there was no need for me to fight the end-of-Thanksgiving airport frenzy. How about you?"

"I'm headed to the airport now. Didn't plan as well as you, I guess."

She waited. What was going on? What had changed since he'd arrived? Something had. Something in a big way.

She'd buried her pain for months, waiting for him to recover, and this is what she got? Mixed messages? Passive-aggressive behavior?

Riley raced toward them, Jess and Keith and another man right behind.

She turned to Daniel. What was she supposed to say? "Well, I guess I'll see you next month at the wedding. Have a safe trip home." She looked away, her eyes stinging, throat swelling, heart thundering. She couldn't be with him a moment longer. And she had no idea how she would survive the wedding and all the various events that went with it.

She still loved him, and that was that. But apparently she would have to fall out of love.

"Papa!" Riley leaped into Daniel's arms. "Are you coming home with us?"

"Sorry, bud. I've got to be back at work tomorrow. Keith's friend is taking me to the airport now. I'll see you in a month, though, and I'll stick around for a while over the Christmas break. Okay?"

"O-kay," he said, resignation in his voice. "I love you, Papa."

"I love you, too, bud," he said, his voice tight. He gave Jess a quick hug then, and shook Keith's hand. He looked at Maureen.

"Aren't you going to hug Gramster?"

"We already said goodbye," Maureen said. She headed out the front door, swallowing hard, blinking fast.

In the car Riley made sure there were no lags in conversation on the drive to Keith's house, a magnificent home in the Hollywood Hills. She managed to say good-night to everyone, then headed for the guest room. Item by item she tore her clothes off and staggered to the shower. It was her turn to mourn, and mourn him she did, hitting her fists against the tile, the water pouring down on her, tears flowing unchecked, her heart squeezing into a tight fist, denied love, denied the man she loved. She'd been waiting and waiting. What a dreamer she'd been. She had come to believe in knights in shining armor, after all. Now she had to acknowledge the fantasy.

She finally dragged herself out of the shower and fell into bed, her hair wet, her heart heavy. But tomorrow was a new day. Whatever hope she'd been secreting away died. She would find someone to love again, someone who would love her back. Once she set her mind to something, she could do anything. Anything at all.

Even replace Daniel Cregg.

CHAPTER 21

There's no place like home, Maureen thought, as her taxi pulled up in front of her house the next afternoon. The cab driver jumped out, grabbed her suitcases from the trunk and set them on the sidewalk. She passed him some bills, picked up her bags and headed toward her gate.

"I'll get those for you."

She looked toward the voice, saw Daniel sitting at the top of her stairs. He stood, looking even worse than he had the night before. She clamped down on the temptation to pull him into her arms and say everything would be okay. "What are you doing here?"

"We didn't get to finish our conversation."

"You mean *you* didn't finish our conversation." She refused to let him off the hook.

He nodded.

"I thought you had to work today, Daniel."

He opened her gate and took her suitcases. "I blew it off. I had a layover in San Francisco, then I just didn't get back on the plane."

Everything she did was by rote—climb the stairs, put the

key in the lock, open the door, go inside. She intentionally dulled her response to seeing him.

He slid the suitcases inside the doorway but didn't cross the threshold. He wanted to finish their conversation in her open doorway?

"Would you take a ride with me?" he asked.

"Where?"

"I'd like to see your magical place where you think things through and make decisions. Take me there? Please?"

No matter how hard she tried to keep hope at bay, it crept in. She tried to beat it back, but it kept marching, pounding rhythmically, a driving cadence in her head and heart. "Let me grab my car keys."

Neither of them spoke during the journey, the tension as thick and hot as sauna steam. Only when they'd made the short climb from where they parked to the spot where she liked to sit did he speak, not looking at her but at the horizon. It was cold and windy, with whitecaps dotting the Bay. She hadn't come prepared for the weather. She pulled her sweater closer.

"I can see why you like it here," he said.

"What do you want, Daniel?"

He waited a couple of beats. "Have you been dating, Maureen?"

"I don't see how that's your business."

"Fair enough. I haven't, by the way."

"Why not?"

"I didn't know why until last night."

"Last night you said you missed me, then you asked me how work was."

"That's because last night I finally came to understand everything."

"What's everything?"

"I've been grieving."

"Yes, I know."

"You do? Well, I hadn't put that word to it until last night. I didn't realize you could grieve for someone who still lived. And not just Jess and Riley, but you. Especially you. I thought I could handle seeing you again. Then I saw you. The words that came out? I hadn't planned them, had no control over them." He blew out a breath. "I'm in love with you, Maureen. I want— No, I need to be with you. No job is worth not having you. If it means my moving to San Francisco—or Los Angeles, for that matter—I'll do it. I'm your man."

Maureen crumbled. She'd been holding herself in check for so long, waiting for the words, hoping against hope. Now she fell into his arms, feeling his come around her, strong and comforting and loving.

"I love you, too, Daniel. Oh, how much I love you." She pressed kisses to his face until he cupped hers, steadied her and kissed her soundly. "I'll move to Seattle," she said against his mouth.

His arms tightened. He pressed his forehead to hers. "Marry me. Please marry me."

"Yes. Yes, yes, yes."

"You don't want to move to L.A.?" he asked.

"I've thought about it a lot. It's time for Jess to live her own life. We'll be there for her. We'll visit a lot, and Riley can come during vacations to stay with us—he's going to need us to protect him from the Hollywood influence, you know. But it's time for us just to be his grandparents," she finished.

"Do you still want another child?" he asked, moving back a little.

"Yes, but I can live without it, too."

"I want a child."

She hadn't thought she could be happier, but he'd proved her wrong. "Then I'm your woman, Daniel Cregg. For life."

"For life, my sweet Maureen. For life."

He kissed her again as the cold wind swirled around them, and the city stretched before them like their future—magnificent and infinite.

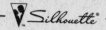

SPECIAL EDITION™

**brings you a heartwarming
new McKettrick's story from**

NEW YORK TIMES BESTSELLING AUTHOR

LINDA LAEL MILLER

THE McKETTRICK
Way

Meg McKettrick is surprised to be reunited
with her high school flame, Brad O'Ballivan,
who has returned home to his family's
neighboring ranch. After seeing Meg again,
Brad realizes he still loves her. But the pride
of both manage to interfere with love...until
an unexpected matchmaker gets involved.

—— McKettrick Women ——

Available December wherever you buy books.

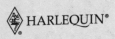

HARLEQUIN®

American ★ Romance®

Kate Merrill had grown up convinced
that the most attractive men were incapable
of ever settling down. Yet the harder she
resisted the superstar photographer
Tyler Nichols, the more persistent the
handsome world traveler became.
So by the time Christmas arrived, there
was only one wish on her holiday list—
that she was wrong!

LOOK FOR

THE CHRISTMAS DATE

BY

Michele Dunaway

**Available December
wherever you buy books**

REQUEST YOUR FREE BOOKS!

2 FREE NOVELS PLUS 2 FREE GIFTS!

There's the life you planned. And there's what comes next.™

YES! Please send me 2 FREE Harlequin® NEXT™ novels and my 2 FREE mystery gifts. After receiving them, if I don't wish to receive any more books, I can return the shipping statement marked "cancel." If I don't cancel, I will receive 4 brand-new novels every other month and be billed just $3.99 per book in the U.S. or $4.74 per book in Canada, plus 25¢ shipping and handling per book plus applicable taxes, if any.* That's a savings of over 25% off the cover price! I understand that accepting the 2 free books and gifts places me under no obligation to buy anything. I can always return a shipment and cancel at any time. Even if I never buy anything from Harlequin, the two free books and gifts are mine to keep forever.

155 HDN EL33   355 HDN EL4F

Name	(PLEASE PRINT)	
Address		Apt. #
City	State/Prov.	Zip/Postal Code

Signature (if under 18, a parent or guardian must sign)

Order online at www.TryNEXTNovels.com

Or mail to the **Harlequin Reader Service®:**

IN U.S.A.: P.O. Box 1867, Buffalo, NY 14240-1867
IN CANADA: P.O. Box 609, Fort Erie, Ontario L2A 5X3

Not valid to current Harlequin NEXT subscribers.

Want to try two free books from another line?
Call 1-800-873-8635 or visit www.morefreebooks.com

* Terms and prices subject to change without notice. NY residents add applicable sales tax. Canadian residents will be charged applicable provincial taxes and GST. This offer is limited to one order per household. All orders subject to approval. Credit or debit balances in a customer's account(s) may be offset by any other outstanding balance owed by or to the customer. Please allow 4 to 6 weeks for delivery.

Your Privacy: Harlequin Books is committed to protecting your privacy. Our Privacy Policy is available online at www.eHarlequin.com or upon request from the Harlequin Reader Service. From time to time we make our lists of customers available to reputable firms who may have a product or service of interest to you. If you would prefer we not share your name and address, please check here. ☐

NEXT07R

Inside ROMANCE

Stay up-to-date on all your romance reading news!

Inside Romance is a FREE quarterly newsletter highlighting our upcoming series releases and promotions.

Visit

www.eHarlequin.com/InsideRomance

to sign up to receive our complimentary newsletter today!

IRN1107

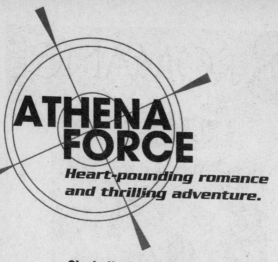

ATHENA FORCE

Heart-pounding romance and thrilling adventure.

She's their ace in the hole.

Posing as a glamorous high roller, Bethany James, a professional gambler and sometimes government agent, uncovers a mob boss's deadly secrets…and the ugly sins from his past. But when a daredevil with a tantalizing drawl calls her bluff, the stakes—and her heart rate—become much, much higher. Beth can't help but wonder: Have the cards been finally stacked against her?

ATHENA FORCE

Will the women of Athena unravel Arachne's powerful web of blackmail and death…or succumb to their enemies' deadly secrets?

Look for

STACKED DECK

by *Terry Watkins.*

Available December wherever you buy books.

HARLEQUIN®

Next™

COMING NEXT MONTH

#97 THREE WISE WOMEN: A Christmas Anthology •
Donna Birdsell, Lisa Childs and Susan Crosby
Here are three unforgettable stories of women drowning in
all the glad tidings, good cheer—and stress!—of the season.
And even if a tall, dark stranger doesn't top their Christmas
lists, it may be just what Santa ordered…so watch as these
women wise up to love in the holidays!

#98 ANNIE ON THE LAM: A CHRISTMAS CAPER
• Jennifer Archer
When the bloom goes off the magnolia, Southern heiress
Annie Macy comes to New York for a new lease on life—
and runs smack-dab into her new boss's money-laundering
scheme. Filching the files that prove his guilt during
the office Christmas party lands her in hot water, until
handsome P.I. Joe Brady leads Annie to safety…by way of
the mistletoe.